WEDNESDAY WEEKS

and the Tower of Shadows

WEDNESDAY WEEKS

and the Tower of Shadows

DENIS KNIGHT  CRISTY BURNE

LOTHIAN
Children's Books

A Lothian Children's Book
Published in Australia and New Zealand in 2021
by Hachette Australia
Level 17, 207 Kent Street, Sydney NSW 2000
www.hachettechildrens.com.au

10 9 8 7 6 5 4 3 2 1

 A catalogue record for this book is available from the National Library of Australia

ISBN 978 0 7344 2019 0 (paperback)

Cover design by Liz Seymour
Cover illustration by Chris Wahl
Author photo courtesy Jessica Wyld
Typeset by Bookhouse, Sydney
Printed and bound in Great Britain by Clays Ltd, Elcograf S.p.A.

 The paper this book is printed on is certified against the Forest Stewardship Council® Standards. McPherson's Printing Group holds FSC® chain of custody certification SA-COC-005379. FSC® promotes environmentally responsible, socially beneficial and economically viable management of the world's forests.

For our families.

Because true magic comes from the heart.

CHAPTER 1

I hold my breath as Alfie's robot zips across the classroom floor. Wheels spinning, it races into the maze and takes the first corner without slowing down. Left! Right! Right! Left! The little purple robot navigates the wooden block corridors with reckless speed.

When it reaches the exit it beeps twice, flashes its lights and does a triumphant bunny hop over the finish line. Then, whistling a cheery tune, it buzzes around Mrs Glock's desk, rockets past the line of fire extinguishers, dodges an attempt by Colin Murphy to catch it in a wastepaper basket, and finishes with a victory lap around our class model of the Harbour Bridge.

Alfie picks up the robot and gives it a pat. 'Great work, Alfie Junior! That was totally molten!' He turns to me and grins like he's just won a lifetime supply of chocolate. 'See, Wednesday? I told you it was easy.'

I roll my eyes. 'Alfie, you know I love you, right?'

And before you start, I don't mean it like *that*. Obviously.

Alfie knows what I mean. 'Of course you do,' he says, spreading his arms wide. His white school shirt is buttoned all the way to the top, he has a hankie folded in his top pocket, and his black hair sticks up like the bristles on a brush. 'What's not to love?'

Alfie's my best friend – okay, technically my only friend – and I know it's not his fault he's a genius. But sometimes – especially times like now, when my whole future is on the line and I'm trying to concentrate – I wish he could dial it back a little. That's all. You know, just a smidge.

I just don't know how to tell him without coming across like a total grouch.

I let out a sigh. 'Never mind.'

I look down at my own blue robot, sitting motionless on the carpet. Apart from the colour, it's identical to Alfie Junior – like a rectangular grapefruit with eyes and four-wheel-drive tyres. I know I'll never be able to get my robot to perform like Alfie's, but that's okay. I don't need it to do anything fancy. All I need to do is get it through the maze. Or, at least, past the second corner. Mrs Glock told us everyone who gets past the second corner will pass the assessment.

'Well done, Alfie,' Mrs Glock says in her singsong voice. 'Perfect, as always.'

'Yeah, perfect,' Colin Murphy mutters. 'A perfect dork.'

Allie Crenshaw sniggers, but Mrs Glock doesn't even look up. She's busy making a note on her shiny black tablet – probably giving Alfie an A-triple-plus with extra credit. Again.

I turn and give Colin one of my special glares – the kind that makes people nervously check their hair, just to make sure it's not on fire. He's a tough-looking kid with buzz-cut hair and a nose that's about half a size bigger than the rest of his face. He prides himself on not being afraid of anything, but in the face of my blazing-hot glare of death he flinches and looks away.

Mrs Glock looks up from her tablet. 'And last but not least . . .' Her eyes land on me and her lips pinch tight. 'Ah, yes. Wednesday.'

I take a deep breath. This is it. My absolute final chance, especially after last week. We were studying chemical reactions. All I had to do was mix bicarb and vinegar to bubble up enough carbon dioxide to extinguish a candle. Instead, my candle shot up like a rocket and set fire to the ceiling.

If I don't pass robotics, I'll flunk science. And that means I'll flunk Year Six. And no way am I repeating the whole 'weird girl tries to fit in' routine with a new year group.

I sneak a peek at the coding app on my laptop where I've been assembling the coloured code blocks that tell my robot what to do. But instead of coloured blocks, the screen is filled with dancing monkeys, flying puppies and what appears to be a portrait of Elvis drinking coffee.

Not again. The bottom drops from my stomach and I hit the button to blank the screen before Mrs Glock can see. Every piece of technology I touch turns to some sort of nightmare, and Mrs Glock knows it. She just doesn't know why.

'All set,' I say, forcing a smile onto my face.

Mrs Glock eyes my screen with suspicion. 'Actually, Wednesday, it's nearly lunchtime,' she says, though the bell is still fifteen minutes away. 'I was thinking it might be best if you skip today's assessment.' She gives me a chilly smile of her own. 'For your own safety, of course.'

My own safety. Yeah, right.

Mrs Glock might act like she's on my side, but I know she's just itching for an excuse to dump me out of her class and send me back to Year Five. Actually, after that whole eyebrow thing last term, I'm pretty sure she'd send me back to kindergarten if she could.

I imagine Mum and Dad's faces if Mrs Glock calls them in for yet another chat. My parents are great – really, they are. But the strain of raising a child with constant fireball issues is starting to get to them.

Luckily, I have a cunning plan.

I'm going to beg.

'Please, Mrs Glock?' I beg. *'Pleeease?* Just give me one more chance. This won't be like the last time, I promise.'

Mrs Glock arches a carefully pencilled eyebrow. 'Like the last seven times, you mean?'

Uh-oh. My cunning plan is running into some early resistance. I push my face into an expression of innocent surprise. 'Seven? Are you sure?'

Mrs Glock's not buying it. 'Quite sure.'

'Hmm.' I frown and start racking my brain for a new plan. 'That seems kind of high.'

'No, Wednesday,' Alfie says helpfully, 'it's definitely seven. Remember?'

I stifle a groan. I should have known this would happen – Alfie's a complete sucker for anything involving numbers. He starts ticking off my list of robot-related disasters on his fingers.

'You've had three blackouts, two meltdowns, one spontaneous electrical discharge and one, um . . . inexplicable rain of fireballs.' Alfie smiles and shakes his head. 'Boy, remember that one?'

Mrs Glock's face twitches and her hand makes an involuntary movement towards the large red fire extinguisher sitting on the corner of her desk. 'I remember,' she says in a voice like ice.

I glare at Alfie, then quickly look away before *his* hair catches on fire.

'Yes, well,' I say, trying desperately to regroup. 'My point is, this time won't be anything like those times.'

'Oh?' Mrs Glock looks unconvinced. 'And why is that?'

'Um . . .' I reach up to touch my own hair, feeling for the special ice-blue streak that seems to have a mind of its own. The rest of my hair is dark brown and totally ordinary, but that streak? It's more like an early warning system than actual hair. Right now it's sitting flat on my head, which is a good sign. 'Because this time I'll be extra, extra careful?'

Mrs Glock shakes her head. She doesn't understand about my hair. 'I'm sorry, Wednesday. Not today.'

My heart sinks into my boots. Kindergarten, here I come.

But then Alfie pipes up again. And this time – amazingly – he's actually being helpful. 'Come on, Mrs G,' he says. 'It's not Wednesday's fault. She's just . . .'

'Careless?' Mrs Glock prompts.

Alfie thinks about it, then shakes his head. 'No.'

'Thoughtless?'

'No.'

'Impulsive?'

'No.'

'Hey!' I protest. 'I'm sitting right here.'

They both ignore me.

Alfie's face lights up as he finds the right words. 'Technologically challenged.'

'Yes, well.' Mrs Glock looks like she's been chewing lemons. 'She certainly is that. Which is why I think it would be best if—'

'Please, Mrs G.' Alfie hits Mrs Glock with the full force of his gigawatt smile. 'I'll keep an eye on her. And if anything gets fried, I'll patch it right up.'

You gotta love Alfie. I mean, here's a kid who lives in a super-busy house with his mum, his dad, his nani, and about a million brothers, sisters and pets. Which means he has totally perfected the art of Getting Adult Attention. And, okay, so he actually has just one brother, two sisters, three cats and a dog, but compared to my zero siblings and one cranky lizard named Spike, it may as well be a million.

In the face of Alfie's relentless enthusiasm, Mrs Glock is helpless. She throws up her hands. 'Oh, all right.'

'Thanks, Mrs G,' Alfie says. 'You're the best! Isn't she, Wednesday?'

I somehow manage to prevent my eyes from rolling so far back in my head that I can see my own brain.

'Yeah, right,' I mutter. 'The best.'

Mrs Glock returns to perch on the edge of her desk – a position which gives her a clear view of the maze and, coincidentally, puts her within easy reach of at least four fire extinguishers.

'Well, go ahead, Wednesday,' she says. 'Let's get this over with.'

Yeah, thanks, Mrs G. Great pep talk.

I take a deep breath and check my laptop. The screen's normal again – no dancing monkeys, no flying puppies, no caffeinated Elvis. Just the coding app, and the sequence of coloured blocks to tell my robot what to do. A blue block to drive forward. An orange block to stop at a corner. Another set of blocks to decide which way to turn. And one more to keep repeating the whole thing until it reaches the exit. A robotic recipe for navigating a maze.

Simple, right? I cross my fingers and click the *Go* button.

For a second, nothing happens. Then my robot lurches into motion. Slowly at first, then more confidently, it trundles forward and enters the maze.

I hold my breath.

My robot reaches the first corner.

It stops.

Waits.

And then . . .

After what seems like an eternity, my robot turns left and starts moving forward again, heading for the second corner.

A warm feeling washes over me. It's working. I'm actually going to pass science. I won't have to—

Out of the corner of my eye, I spot Colin Murphy. He's sneaking up behind Alfie, and he has the wastepaper basket in his hands.

'Hey!' Anger spikes my gut. 'Back off!'

The words are out before I know it. I clamp my lips, but it's too late.

With an ear-splitting electronic squawk, my robot slams into reverse. It accelerates backwards across the floor, then launches into the air like a cruise missile – straight at Colin Murphy's head.

Luckily for Colin, his reflexes are the quickest thing about him. He jams the bin on Alfie's head, then dives for cover. The robot skims his buzz cut, ricochets off the ceiling, and cannons into the Harbour Bridge at about half the speed of light.

CHAPTER 2

It took our class a whole term to build that bridge. It takes half a second for my robot to destroy it. Stripy plastic straws and paperclips explode everywhere. The wreckage falls to the floor around the robot, lies still for a moment, and then quietly bursts into flames.

Thanks to last week's chemistry lesson, I know exactly what's required. Bicarb and vinegar, right? But Mrs Glock goes straight for the big guns. She snatches up the nearest fire extinguisher and kills the blaze with a short, sharp blast of carbon dioxide.

A few seconds tick by in stunned silence. Then Allie Crenshaw uncorks her epic laugh – the one that sounds like a donkey going through a woodchipper – and suddenly everyone's laughing and talking at once.

Well, almost everyone. Colin Murphy picks himself up like a shell-shocked soldier. Alfie has the dented wire wastepaper basket jammed on top of his head like a medieval helmet, but he doesn't seem to notice. He's staring at the melted mess of blue plastic that used to be my robot.

Mrs Glock fixes me with an icy glare, then makes a note on her tablet.

It doesn't take a genius to figure out what it says. I think I'm going to cry.

But then something happens that turns my misery to exasperation.

The lights flicker and a sudden chill fills the air. Every screen in the room goes black. Behind me, I sense a familiar but unwelcome presence.

He's here.

I mean, of course he is. He's been here for almost every other humiliating disaster of the last three years. Why not this one as well?

I turn around.

A tall, shadowy figure stands at the back of the room. Shocked silence spreads through the class like ripples in a pond.

Mrs Glock straightens up like she's been electrocuted. 'Excuse me!' She glares at the cloaked and hooded figure, like she does every time this happens. 'Who are you? And what are you doing in my classroom?'

The figure lowers its hood, revealing a stern face with a pointy grey beard and dark, piercing eyes. 'Forgive the intrusion,' he says in a voice as smooth as chocolate sauce. 'I have come for my apprentice.'

Mrs Glock frowns. 'Apprentice?'

The man flings out a jewelled finger, pointing across the room in a gesture that makes his cloak go all billowy and mysterious.

I mean, seriously. This is the kind of stuff I have to put up with.

Mrs Glock follows the man's finger with her eyes. You can see the moment when she realises he's pointing at me. Her lips go all tight and pinched – it's like her signature move – and her eyes turn hard as marbles.

'Well,' she says. 'I should have known *Wednesday* would be mixed up in this. But *who* are *you*?'

The man's lips curl into a faint smile and he bows. 'As ever, dear lady, I am Abraham Mordecai Weeks, Protector of the Realms, Master of the Seven Transformations, Custodian of the Five Ungovernable Charms, Arch-Excellency Order Enchanter, Wonder Warlock, and Black Belt Magician to the Queen's Royal Order.' He turns to me and beckons. 'Come, Apprentice. We have work to do.'

I fold my arms. I'm pretty sure at least two of his fancy titles are made up. And I'm a hundred per cent not keen on mine.

'Grandpa,' I say. 'Do we have to do this every time?'

Alfie pushes his way to the front of the mystified crowd. He's still wearing the wastepaper basket, pushed

12

back on his head at a rather jaunty angle, and he looks like he's about to burst. 'Molten! You're Wednesday's grandpa? She's told me about you.'

The truth is, Alfie and Grandpa have already met, loads of times. Same goes for Mrs Glock, and for everyone else in my class. They just don't remember.

Grandpa fixes Alfie with an intimidating stare. 'Has she, indeed?' He doesn't seem to notice anything unusual about Alfie's choice of headgear, but then again, post-seventeenth-century fashion isn't really his thing.

Alfie nods, not intimidated in the slightest. He never is. 'Oh, yeah. Like how you're all into magic and stuff? Oh!' His eyes go wide and he takes a coin out of his pocket. 'I've been practising. Here, watch, watch, watch!'

Alfie does a magic trick with the coin, making it disappear from one hand, and then pulling it out of Colin Murphy's ear with the other.

Colin tries to slap Alfie's hand away, but his heart doesn't seem to be in it.

'Bazinga!' Alfie says with a grin.

The class groans. To be fair, it's not a bad trick, but Alfie's been working on it for ages, and we've all seen it a million times.

'Most impressive, young man,' Grandpa says. 'But true magic is more than mere sleight of hand. True magic comes from the heart.' He reaches for the coin. 'Allow me.'

13

With a flourish, he tosses the coin into the air. It spins upwards and then stops, hovering like a UFO. Grandpa claps his hands and the coin disappears in a shower of golden sparkles. The class *oohs* and *aahs* in amazement.

'Where'd it go?' Alfie asks.

Grandpa gestures at Colin. 'If you'd care to check your associate's ear once more . . .'

Alfie reaches for Colin's ear, but before he can get there, Grandpa mutters a word. Colin's eyes bug out as thousands of coins start pouring out of his ear. The class goes nuts, cheering and clapping and diving forward to scoop up the money.

I shake my head. Grandpa's such a show-off. There was so little magic in the spells he just cast, I could barely feel them. A simple levitation charm, a disappearing spell, and a drop of winkleberry juice is all it took to have the whole class eating out of his hand.

He turns to me with a smug expression. 'I'd like to see one of your electrified adding machines do *that*, Apprentice.'

Yeah, I tried to explain computers to Grandpa once. So there's an hour of my life I'll never get back. Not to mention a perfectly good laptop.

Mrs Glock steps forward, slipping and sliding on the torrent of coins still pouring out of Colin's ear. 'Mr Weeks! Please! I really must insist that you—'

'Enough of this foolishness.' Grandpa waves his hand.

This time I can feel it. The spell ripples through the air, freezing Mrs Glock and the rest of the class, and suddenly Grandpa and I are standing in a room full of statues.

'Grandpa!' I scramble over the coins to stand in front of him. 'What are you doing here? I'm trying to pass science. Seriously, you could not have picked a worse time.'

Grandpa gives me a lofty smile. 'Time is immaterial, my young apprentice.'

I prop my hands on my hips. 'Firstly, I'm not your apprentice.'

If my defiance bothers him, he doesn't show it. 'And yet, you are. Destined to—'

'And secondly, if time is so immaterial, then why can't you—'

'Also,' Grandpa interrupts regally, 'when in public, you should address me as Master.'

'*Master?*' I fold my arms and glare at him as the lunch bell starts to ring. 'No, nope. Forget it.'

Grandpa shrugs and closes his eyes. The enormous ruby ring on his right hand starts to glow. He gestures with his right arm, as if opening a curtain, and suddenly an inky black void appears, floating in mid-air like a doorway into a black hole.

'Time to depart,' he says. 'Come along, Apprentice Protector.'

He steps into the void and disappears.

I look around with a sigh. The only thing I want to protect is my social life. Despite the bell, Mrs Glock and the rest of the class are still frozen like statues. But they won't stay that way much longer. When the spell wears off, the coins will be gone, lunchtime will be nearly over, and nobody will remember Grandpa's visit at all.

Of course, with my luck, Mrs Glock will still remember to give me a final science grade, and considering the destroyed bridge and melted robot, it will almost certainly be an F.

I trudge through the doorway and into the void.

CHAPTER 3

If there's one thing I hate more than wading through waist-deep slugs, it's wading through waist-deep slugs with my smug magical know-it-all grandfather hassling me every five seconds.

'Anything, Apprentice?' he asks for the thousandth time. He's hovering next to me just above slug height, sitting cross-legged like some sort of carpetless genie.

I shuffle through the endless swamp of bright pink slugs, shoes and socks in hand, feeling with my toes. Apart from the smell, which is pretty much as bad as you'd expect, it's a bit like wading through a giant bowl of strawberry pudding. Except strawberry pudding doesn't try to slime its way into your underwear. And speaking of strawberry pudding, I'm way overdue for lunch.

'Nothing yet,' I say. 'And don't call me "Apprentice". I have a name, you know.'

'Less talk, Apprentice.' Grandpa stares loftily into the distance. 'Time is of the essence.'

Apparently, other people's grandpas bring them sweets and read them stories. Mine drags me through the Nine Realms of space and time because a sword told him I'm destined to save the universe. Go figure, right?

And it's not like I'm even good at it. I suck at magic. It would be cool if I could do even half of what Grandpa can do, like levitate or turn into a raven, but you know what? Protecting the realms from unimaginable evil doesn't seem all that important right now. I'd rather have friends, and a passing grade from Mrs Glock.

I concentrate on pushing through the slugs with my bare toes, feeling for the telltale prickle of a winkleberry. I mean, I get that they're rare and vital ingredients, found only in this swamp. I just don't get why we have to search for them right now, in the middle of lunchtime.

'Seriously, Grandpa,' I say. 'How can I protect the realms if I can't even pass science?'

Grandpa gives me a serious look, and for a wild and unimaginable second, I think he's going to give me a serious answer. But then he asks, 'What is the magical property of the winkleberry?'

I let out a sigh. All he cares about is protecting the realms. We've covered this topic a million times, along with the properties of dozens of other magical ingredients. 'Multiplication.'

'Precisely.' Grandpa nods. 'The power of the winkleberry lies not in its own properties, but in its ability to temporarily multiply the properties of other ingredients. One drop of winkleberry juice, and a weak spell becomes powerful. A small quantity of an ingredient becomes greater.'

'And a thousand coins come out of Colin Murphy's ear instead of only one,' I say. 'Whoop-de-doo.'

Grandpa frowns. 'This is not a game, Wednesday. As Protector of the Realms, you will one day be engaged in a centuries-old battle between—'

'I know, I know,' I say, interrupting Grandpa's centuries-old story about whatever centuries-old battle is going to be won by me wading around in a swamp. Seriously, before he showed up, I'd been having such a beautifully normal life. Mostly.

The ironic thing is, when Grandpa first appeared out of nowhere at our dining table on meatloaf night three years ago, he was all like, 'Don't worry, Wednesday, I can teach you to control your magic.' And yet here I am, up to my waist in slugs and further from a normal life than ever.

Ever since that fateful meatloaf night, Grandpa's been living in our basement. Thanks to his handy dandy amnesia spell, Mum thinks he's Dad's grandfather, and Dad thinks he's Mum's grandfather. He claims to be my great-great-great-great-grandfather, or some number of greats, but as you've probably already gathered, he's quite big on being great.

Grandpa says I'm the first in seven generations to develop the magical power, that I'm tasked with becoming the next Protector of the Realms, and that – oh, by the way – the entire future of the universe depends on him yanking me out of class whenever he feels like it.

He also says that the reason I'm having so much trouble with my magic is because I should have started training when I was three. He would have stopped by sooner, but so sorry, he's been busy fighting in the Goblin Wars and saving the universe from a Third Age of Never-Ending Darkness or whatever.

Yeah, right. Third age of napping in the sun, more like it.

'Why now?' I ask. 'What's so important that you have to keep barging in every second day and dragging me out of class? I'm trying to have a life, you know.'

'Ah, yes.' Grandpa's eyes gleam. 'A life.' He says *life* in a way that makes it seem like growing cacti and feeding mealworms to Spike don't count. 'You wish to control your magic, do you not?'

'Of course I do.' I swipe my foot through the slime with enough force to send a wave of slugs squelching across my thighs. 'But that doesn't mean you have to drag me out of class and wipe everyone's memories on the way out! Can't it wait until the weekend, or—'

'No!' Grandpa's eyes blaze and he smacks a fist down into his open palm, causing his invisible perch to wobble alarmingly. 'It cannot wait. Every day that passes brings us closer to . . .'

He stops suddenly, like he's afraid of saying too much.

'Closer to what?' I ask. Because I'm a little bit tired of training every other day for a future that may never come, in a discipline I can't grasp, to battle an evil I really can't see right now. Maybe this time he'll finally let me in on the big secret.

But, no. The fire fades from Grandpa's eyes and he simply says, 'Closer to the time when you *must* be ready.'

I sigh. Grandpa says the only difference between a good sorcerer and an evil one is what they do with their power. And what do I do with my power? Does accidentally blowing things up count as good or evil?

A sudden lance of pain in the ball of my foot brings my mind back to the swamp. Ouch. Feels like a winkleberry, all right. I'd recognise that stabbing pain anywhere. It's almost as bad as stepping on Lego.

I reach deep into the slugs and pull out a prickly, cherry-sized ball. One of Grandpa's beloved winkleber-ries. A ripe one, too, by the look of its lime-green spots.

'Got one,' I announce, throwing my fist into the air like I've just won the Faery Solstice Cup.

I wait for Grandpa to acknowledge my rare success, but instead he's staring out across the pink waves of the swamp. There's an odd expression on his face, like he's forgotten something, and for a second he looks less like a Queen's Black Belt Magician and more like a frazzled old man.

'Grandpa?'

'Silence,' he commands, his lost expression lifting. 'I hear something.'

All I can hear is the non-stop slither of slug on slug. Which is hardly surprising – the Realm of Slugs isn't exactly a bustling metropolis. I really prefer the Realm of Dragons, which has an awesome toasted sandwich shop, or the Realm of Unfriendly Cats, which isn't as unfriendly as it sounds, especially if you like cats. But we've been to the Realm of Slugs loads of times and never met another living thing. Except the slugs, of course.

'We're being followed,' Grandpa whispers.

I frown. It's normal for Grandpa to get distracted by his spell books or some foul-smelling potion, but this is ridiculous. There's nothing but slugs from here to the horizon. If anyone was following us, we'd see them.

Suddenly, Grandpa dives, plunging into the sea of slugs and vanishing with an almighty slurp.

Huh. He's never done *that* before.

I shove the winkleberry in the pocket of my school uniform and wade over to the spot where he disappeared, doing my best to feel around under the glop. 'Grandpa?'

He's gone.

22

I wait. Scan the glistening pink surface of the swamp for ripples.

There's nothing.

I fold my arms and wait some more. Everything's quiet – except for the slithering, which really gets on your nerves after a while.

I swallow hard. He's been under the slugs for a long time. What if something's happened? What if he's hurt, or doesn't come back?

I'm starting to panic when there's an almighty commotion and a giant slug-covered monster rises from the swamp.

It has two heads.

Actually, scratch that. It's two monsters, one head each.

The monsters gasp for breath and wipe away slugs. One of them is wearing a cloak – Grandpa – and I have to say he does not look good in that much sluggy pink. The other one is wearing a soggy schoolbag and a dented wire wastepaper basket, and he's beaming like a lighthouse.

It's Alfie.

CHAPTER 4

'Hey, Wednesday. How's it going?' Alfie pulls a bright pink slug out of his ear and flicks it away. It doesn't seem to bother him that he's completely coated with a thick layer of slime. 'And whoa, Wednesday's grandpa! You totally owned it, swimming at me like that, all Loch Ness Monster and stuff.'

'Alfie!' I have so many questions right now. But I decide to start with the basics. 'How'd you get here?'

'How, indeed?' Grandpa rakes a handful of slugs from his beard, then flicks his hand. '*Expurgo spiritum!*' he says, and the slugs drop from his body, leaving him clean and dry. 'We are, after all, in another dimension.'

Apparently, most ordinary people simply aren't equipped to cope with the idea that there are nine unique realms, all co-existing in a multi-dimensional universe, and that humans occupy only one. Which is why Grandpa is so quick with his amnesia spell, and why it's such a mystery how Alfie came to be swimming with the slugs.

Alfie smiles and tugs at his normally spiky hair, now slicked flat with translucent pink mucus. 'Too easy. After you did all that hocus-pocus stuff back at school, I slipped into the black shadow thingy behind you. What is it, like a wormhole or something?'

Grandpa frowns. 'That "hocus-pocus stuff", as you call it, is one of the finest amnesia charms in all the Nine Realms.'

'An amnesia charm?' Alfie's eyes light up. 'I knew it! I knew you could do magic. Not just coin tricks and stuff. Real, actual magic!' He turns to me, quivering with excitement. 'And Wednesday! You're his apprentice? How cool is that!'

My mouth drops open. 'You knew?'

'Well, sure.' Alfie shrugs. 'It's kind of obvious when you think about it. The blackouts, the meltdowns, the fireballs. Mrs Glock's eyebrows. And how else could your grandpa do that thing with Colin's ear?' He grins. 'I mean, a thousand coins? Come on.'

'Yes, well.' Grandpa clears his throat. 'That still doesn't explain your immunity to my spell.'

Alfie's grin grows even wider. 'I'm guessing we've got my old mate Colin Murphy to thank for that.' He taps

25

his makeshift helmet. 'If metal mesh can stop electro-magnetic rays, maybe it can stop magic too.'

'This?' Grandpa removes the wastepaper basket from Alfie's head and examines it with a deeply sceptical look. 'Impossible. I detect no enchantment.'

I roll my eyes. 'It's not magic, Grandpa. It's science.'

'Nonsense.' Grandpa shakes his head. 'I'm sure there's a perfectly rational explanation. Something in his horoscope, perhaps.'

Alfie slips off his slime-coated schoolbag. 'So where are we, anyway?' He looks around the Realm of Slugs with keen interest. 'Do you guys swim here often? I mean, it's not exactly—'

'Why'd you bring your backpack?' I ask, incredulous.

Alfie smiles. 'Well, I'm travelling through a wormhole to another dimension, right? So, I just thought, maybe I'll need a snack. And it's good to stay hydrated. Plus, Alfie Junior gets lonely without me.' He unzips the schoolbag and peers inside. 'Don't worry, he's fine.' He wipes his hands on a snow-white hankie, then reaches in and pulls out a container of dreamy smelling pastries. 'Samosa?'

'Alfie, you're a genius!' I gratefully take the snack, but Grandpa wrinkles his nose.

Alfie shrugs and takes a big bite. 'Anyway, after that I hid in the slugs. I didn't want to get in the way of the whole sorcerer's apprentice thing you guys had going on.'

'You were under the slugs this whole time?' I try not to choke on my samosa. 'How'd you breathe?'

Alfie holds up something long, thin and stripy. It's a straw from the Harbour Bridge. 'Like this,' he says, sticking one end of the straw in his mouth and puffing in and out.

Grandpa raises an eyebrow. 'A plastic snorkular. Impressive.'

Alfie pulls the straw from his lips. 'Does that mean I can stay?'

Grandpa frowns. 'I'm afraid not.' He raises his hand and I feel a surge as he gathers his magic. 'In fact, it's probably time to—'

'No!' I lunge forward and grab his arm. 'No more amnesia spells.'

Because that's *it*. I've had enough of Grandpa ruining my life. Here, at last, is a friend I can share this stuff with. And there's no way I'm going to let Grandpa mess it up.

'No?' He gives me a stern look from under his shaggy brows.

'I mean it, Grandpa.' I step back and fold my arms. 'If you wipe Alfie's memory again, we're done, okay?'

Alfie blinks. 'Again?'

'No more excursions, no more training,' I tell Grandpa. 'I'm out.'

Grandpa frowns and strokes his beard. But before he can answer, there's a loud glopping sound behind me and I turn to see another slug-covered figure rising from the swamp, accompanied by an eruption of foul-smelling gas.

'Oh, come now.' Grandpa flings up his hands. 'How many of these wastepaper baskets are there?'

But the new arrival doesn't look like any of the kids from school. It's taller than Grandpa – a lot taller – and it's topped with a pair of giant horns. Slugs drop from the creature's flesh. No, wait, it's not flesh. It's some sort of spiky black armour. The horns look like they're built into the creature's helmet.

Alfie drops his straw. 'Molten.'

'Stay back!' Grandpa's voice rings out over the swamp as he raises a hand towards the creature. 'Don't make me destroy you.'

Uh-oh. It looks like Grandpa's preparing to unleash a serious magical butt-kicking on the mysterious newcomer. I step back. I accidentally got in the way of one of these once before, when we were practising magic-carpet wrestling and my phone went off at the wrong time. My hair grew back eventually – the blue streak was untouched, of course – but those carpets will never be the same.

The giant figure stands tall, gripping a huge iron war hammer in its steel-clad right hand. 'Destroy me?' Its deep, booming voice is slightly muffled by the skull-faced visor concealing its face. More carved skulls adorn the black armour at its chest, wrist and knee.

Whoever this guy is, he really has a thing for skulls.

'Come now, Weeks,' the giant rumbles. 'Is that any way to greet an old friend?'

Grandpa peers at the giant, then gasps. 'No! It cannot be. Gorgomoth?'

'That's *King* Gorgomoth to you, Sorcerer.'

'King, indeed.' Grandpa scowls and shakes his head. 'How came you to this place, usurper?'

'Foolish old crow,' Gorgomoth sneers. 'Did you think you were the only one with secrets?' He points to the ring on Grandpa's right hand. 'Now, hand over the goods.'

'My ring? Surely a king has many finer jewels in his collection.'

'Don't play coy with me, old man.' Gorgomoth takes a step closer and raises his war hammer. 'I know about the Stones. That ring and I have a hot date with enslaving the universe. So hand it over, or—'

Without a flicker of warning, the armoured giant slashes his hammer straight down at Grandpa's head. But Grandpa dodges nimbly aside and the hammer splashes down into the swamp, sending slugs flying in all directions.

'Then you leave me no choice,' Grandpa says grimly. He waves me and Alfie back. 'Get behind me, both of you.'

We scramble behind Grandpa and I feel a dizzying surge as he gathers his magic. It swirls around him like a thunderstorm, making his cloak snap and billow.

'In the name of the Nine Masters, I charge you,' Grandpa intones, raising his right hand. 'With the Seven Stones of Saranon, I bind you.' Jewelled rings and amulets glow all over his body, searing green and blue. 'By the power of Undilion, I command you . . . Begone from this place!'

There's a blinding flash, and a bolt of pure white energy erupts from Grandpa's hand.

I've never felt such a powerful blast of magic. I stagger, but Alfie grabs me and keeps me from face-planting into the swamp. The bolt of power rockets through the air and explodes against Gorgomoth's chest, but the armoured giant doesn't even flinch.

Instead, he laughs – a deep, bone-chilling rumble. 'Your powers are weak, old man. Behold!' He snaps his fingers, and suddenly his towering figure is on fire from head to toe with searing, white-hot flames. There's a horrible sizzling sound as a thousand slugs shrivel and burn.

Grandpa staggers back. 'The Unquenchable Fire of Tariel!'

'I think you mean the Unquenchable Fire of Gorgomoth,' the blazing giant sneers.

Grandpa's face turns grim. 'Stolen magic to match a stolen crown! Is there no limit to your greed, O Unclean One?'

'Finders keepers, old fool,' Gorgomoth booms. 'Now, give me the ring.'

'Never!' Grandpa stands tall and proud. 'You may blast me into a thousand pieces, but you shall never have the Ruby Ring.'

Gorgomoth shrugs. 'As you wish.' He raises his hand and hurls a massive fireball.

Grandpa mutters a word. The six green jewels on his belt glow and the fireball explodes against an invisible shield about halfway between him and Gorgomoth.

Gorgomoth laughs. 'Where is your sword, old man? Where is the dreaded Sorcerer's Blade?' He hurls another fireball. It explodes against Grandpa's shield, much closer this time, as if the shield is shrinking from the blasts. 'You still have the belt, I see. But your faith in that broken relic is misplaced. Now, give me the ring.'

Grandpa staggers back. He turns to me, his face etched with fear.

'Run, Wednesday,' he says. 'Run!'

I turn to run, but then I stop. I can't leave Grandpa here, alone with this slug-sizzling, fireball-flinging psycho.

'Come on!' Alfie grabs me and drags me backwards through the slugs.

Grandpa hurls another blinding white bolt of power, but Gorgomoth bats it away. He shoots back with a massive fireball that explodes inches from Grandpa's face, scorching his eyebrows and knocking him off his feet. The jewels on Grandpa's belt go dark.

'No!' I break free of Alfie's grip and start forward, but Grandpa scrambles up again. At first, I think he's going to run with us, to escape. But then he swipes his hand across the sky. The Ruby Ring glows red and an inky black void appears. Genius!

'Quickly, Wednesday,' he says.

I don't need to be told twice. I shove Alfie into the void, then dive in after him. I turn, looking for Grandpa.

He's there, peering into the void from the pink of the swamp. 'Wednesday!' he calls, but he doesn't jump in. Instead, he throws something, and the last thing I see is a flash of red heading straight for me.

'Keep it safe,' Grandpa calls, 'and keep it—'

The void flickers closed.

Without thinking, I catch the flash of red. It's Grandpa's ring.

'Grandpa!' I shout into the nothing. But it's too late. He's gone, and without his ring, he can't get back.

CHAPTER 5

We're in a dark, gloomy place. I'm sticky with slugs. And I can't see a thing.

I peer through the dark, expecting to see Mrs Glock's classroom, with its walls covered in posters, class rules and fire extinguishers. But we're not in Mrs Glock's classroom. Not unless someone's boarded up the windows and turned off the lights.

It does smell kind of familiar, though . . .

I reach for the magic, make a gesture with my hand, and say, 'Light.'

A pale luminous globe of energy manifests inside my cupped hand.

I see Alfie's face, staring wide-eyed at the glowing orb, and beyond him, the familiar surroundings of Grandpa's basement. But no Grandpa.

He's sent us home.

'Whoa!' Alfie says. 'How'd you do that?' Which is funny, because that's exactly what I said to him yesterday, in maths.

Sometimes I forget how cool magic can be, especially if you've never seen it before. Manifesting an orb of light is the first spell Grandpa taught me. He calls it the Luminating Globe of Lost Tarimos. I just call it the Light spell.

I snap my sluggy fingers, and a dozen candles dotted around the room pop into flame. Grandpa and electricity don't get along, which saves on power. On the other hand, our candle bill is through the roof.

I release the magic, and the little glowing orb blinks out.

'Okay, okay, okay.' Alfie takes a deep breath. His eyes look a little wild. 'That was intense. I have four questions.' He looks around the cavernous basement. 'First, where are we?'

'Grandpa's basement,' I tell him.

'What?' Alfie's voice goes high-pitched with astonishment. 'We're in your house?'

'Technically,' I admit. Although, technically, our house never actually had a basement before Grandpa arrived. So it's just as well Mum and Dad never come down here.

Grandpa's basement is big. I mean, it's really big, in a way that's not always readily apparent. The area we're standing in now – the area closest to the long

34

wooden staircase with its seventeen steps of subtly varying height – is Grandpa's living quarters. His bed's unmade, as usual, and there's dishes in the sink and laundry all over the floor, also usual.

Alfie nods. 'Second, what was that slug place? Third, who was that giant burning dude? And fourth, is your grandpa going to be okay?'

'Alfie . . .' There's so much I want to tell him, but there isn't time. 'Give me a minute, all right? I need to think.'

I sink into the ratty old armchair that Grandpa calls his 'Settee of Interdimensional Contemplation'. I don't care that I'm covered in slug-slime. I have way bigger problems right now.

Over the years, Grandpa has taken me to loads of weird magical places where we've seen all kinds of crazy creatures, like fire snakes, frost spiders and self-combusting lava lizards. We even ran across an angry swarm of polymorphic apparition bees once. You don't want one of those things teleporting into your under-pants, believe me.

But we've never come across anything that Grandpa wasn't able to handle.

Until today.

I try to think what to do, but the fear and anger ripping my guts won't let me. If I don't get a grip on myself ASAP, I'm heading straight for another UFI: Unintended Fireball Incident. All I can see is the towering figure of Gorgomoth, and Grandpa's worried face as he threw me the ring.

Wait, that's it! The ring.

I jump out of the armchair. 'I have to go back. Lock the door on your way out, okay?'

'What?' Alfie looks at me in dismay. 'Wednesday, no.'

I swallow hard, remembering the stench as slugs sizzled and burned in Gorgomoth's Unquenchable Fire. How can I go up against that? I don't have any answers. All I know is that Grandpa needs me, and if I don't do everything in my power to help him, I'll never forgive myself.

'He's my grandpa,' I say. 'I have to go.'

Alfie grins and hitches up his backpack. 'Of course you do. And I'm coming with you.'

I shake my head. 'No, you're not.'

'Come on, Wednesday,' Alfie says, doing these big puppy-dog eyes. 'Let me help you on your quest.'

I frown. 'Quest?'

'Sure.' Alfie grins. 'Your heroic quest to rescue your grandpa from the giant burning dude. It'll be awesome! I'll be all like, "Hey Flame Brain! Give us back Wednesday's grandpa!" And you'll be like, "Prepare to meet your doom, burning guy!" It'll be just like the boss battle in *Quest of Heroes III*.'

I step back as Alfie rips out an epic series of air-sword moves, slashing and thrusting at an invisible enemy.

I shake my head. Everything Alfie knows, he's learned from a computer.

'Alfie, this isn't a game,' I tell him.

'I know.' Alfie's face turns serious. 'That's why I can't let you do it alone. Come on, Wednesday. Please?'

For a moment, I'm tempted.

I want to say 'Sure!'

I want to say 'Let's do this thing!'

But I don't want Alfie to get hurt. And it's simply not safe for ordinary humans to dabble in magic.

'Sorry, Alfie,' I tell him. 'Maybe next time.'

I slip the Ruby Ring onto my finger and reach for the magic. Theoretically, this ring can transport me anywhere in the Nine Realms – or at least, anywhere I've already been. I've seen Grandpa use it a thousand times, and he can barely operate a toaster. How hard can it be to open an interdimensional wormhole?

'Wait,' Alfie says. But I don't have time to wait. Grandpa doesn't have time.

I've never done this before – used the ring, I mean – so I'm going to have to start with the basics. According to Grandpa, all magic works the same way. You draw it in, focus your intention, then say a word to release the spell.

Grandpa says the word doesn't matter. He says it's the sorcerer's intention that's important. That you draw the magic with your heart, but you shape it with your mind.

Which is why Grandpa tends to go for fancy-sounding Latin phrases, while I like to keep it a bit simpler.

So I raise my hand, swipe it through the air, and say the first word that pops into my head. '*Open.*'

Nothing happens.

I do it again. 'Open up!'

Still nothing. Which sucks, because how could my intention be any clearer?

Alfie's staring at me like I've lost my marbles, but I'm too worried about Grandpa to feel embarrassed.

Angry sparks burst from the ground as I stamp my foot and swipe the air like a maniac. '*Open!* Come on, you stupid ring. Take me back. *Open!*'

An inky black void resolutely fails to materialise in front of me. Okay, that's it. You want intention? I'll give you intention.

I pull myself up into my most commanding pose. 'BY THE SEVEN STONES OF SARANON,' I bellow at the top of my voice, 'I COMMAND YOU TO *OPEN!*'

There's a moment – a long moment – and then . . .

'If you don't mind,' a dry, dusty voice says from somewhere behind me, 'I'm trying to sleep.'

I spin, searching the room.

All I see is Grandpa's workbench. Its wooden surface is carved with weird runes and sigils, and piled high with wands, cauldrons, alembics and crucibles, as well as strange herbs, fruits, and all the other hard-to-find and mostly disgusting ingredients that Grandpa uses in his potions. The wall behind the workbench is lined with shelves loaded with thick leather-bound volumes of ancient lore, interspersed with skulls, masks, idols, and other arcane souvenirs that Grandpa's accumulated over the years.

There's nobody else in the room.

'W-W-Wednesday?' Alfie stammers. He looks like he's seen a ghost.

'What?'

Alfie points at one of the shelves behind the workbench.

My eyes fall on one of Grandpa's ornaments. It's not one of his more impressive ones – just a plain, ordinary skull. Probably human, although with Grandpa you never know.

I'm surprised Alfie's so freaked out about it. He's seen skulls before, loads of times, at the natural history museum. It must be the after-effects of what we've just been through, combined with the spooky candlelight of the basement.

Mind you, there *is* something a bit strange about this particular skull. I walk closer, peering at it. Something about the way the candlelight flickers across the empty eye sockets makes it seem almost alive.

I look more closely.

'What?' the skull asks, teeth clacking. 'Have I got something on my face?'

'Aaah!' I scream.

'Aaah!' the skull screams, its weathered jawbone gaping wide.

'Aaah!' Alfie screams.

For a moment, everything's quiet. Alfie and I stare at the skull, and the skull stares back. Vivid pinpoints of orange light twinkle inside its eye sockets, giving it an air of eerie intelligence.

'Sorry about that,' the skull says. 'My social skills are a little rusty. I don't get out as much as I used to.'

'Y-you can talk,' I manage.

The pinpoints of light wander upwards in the skull's eye sockets, and I realise it's just rolled its eyes at me. 'Ten points to the young lady in the soggy trousers,' the skull says. 'Want to try for the double?'

'But you're a skull!' Alfie blurts out. 'Skulls can't talk.'

'Ding-ding-ding-ding-ding!' the skull says. 'We have a winner.'

For someone without a face, he sure has a smart mouth. I wonder why Grandpa never told me he had a talking skull. Oh, well. Add that to the list of a million-and-one other sworn secrets he hasn't told me. Which reminds me . . .

'Look, we don't have time to chat,' I tell the skull. 'We have an important rescue mission.'

'A rescue mission?' the skull asks. 'Then you must be Wednesday. What a treat to finally meet you.'

I nod warily. 'And you are?'

The skull's glowing eyes lock onto mine. 'Young lady, if I were to tell you my true name it would blow your eyebrows clean off your face. And I have a strict eyebrow preservation policy.'

'Me too,' I say. 'But, if you'll excuse us, we're in a rush.'

'Looks more like you're in a pickle, if you ask me,' the skull says.

'Look, skull-guy . . .' I begin, but Alfie interrupts.

'We can't call him skull-guy,' he says.

'Well, we have to call him something,' I retort.

'Why don't you call me a taxi?' the skull asks. 'I've had enough of this dreary basement.'

'Let's call him Bruce,' Alfie says.

'Bruce?!' the skull screeches in protest. 'You'd better watch it. I'm starting to rethink my eyebrow policy.'

I sneak a glance at Alfie. He gives me a grin.

'You don't like Bruce?' I say to the skull. 'How about Maurice? Or Dudley? Or Rudolph?'

The skull clamps its jaw tight and starts humming.

I recognise the tune and feel a pang of guilt. It's Grandpa's favourite song, *I Once a Wandering Wizard Knew*. This skull – whatever its name is – has clearly been hanging out with Grandpa way too long.

'How about Alphonse?' I say.

The skull keeps humming, but it's starting to sound desperate. I totally understand why. No one in their right mind, disarticulated skeleton or otherwise, can stand too much of *I Once a Wandering Wizard Knew*.

'How about Skully McSkullface?' Alfie asks.

'Oh, fine.' The skull stops humming and lets out a sigh. 'Bruce, it is. Now, what have you two done with Abraham?'

CHAPTER 6

We fill Bruce the skull in on everything that happened back at the swamp. Alfie pretty much re-enacts the whole fight.

'. . . so then, the big scary burning dude was all like, "The Ruby Ring will be mine!" And Wednesday's grandpa was like, "By the Power of Underpants, I command you!" But the scary dude was like, "Your powers are weak, old man! I'm enslaving the universe!" and then Wednesday's grandpa told us to run, and he did that black shadow thingy, and then we ended up here.'

Somehow, a furrow appears in Bruce's bony brow. 'Are you sure this burning creature mentioned the Ruby Ring?'

'Absolutely.' I hold up my hand, where the ring gleams on my finger. 'He seemed pretty keen to have it.'

'All right,' Bruce says. 'Now, think carefully. Did Abraham call the creature by name?'

'Yep. He called him—' Alfie hesitates.

'Gorgomoth?' Bruce whispers the name like he really hopes it's the wrong one.

I swear I hear a ghostly ripple in the air, and a faint, far-off groaning noise.

I gulp. 'That's the one.'

Bruce clatters his teeth. 'This is bad. This is very, very bad.'

Yeah, no kidding. But at least Alfie and I aren't in it alone anymore. We've got a magical talking skull on our side now, right? I wait for some guidance, some kind of wisdom from beyond the grave, but Bruce says nothing.

I frown. 'Erm, so . . . Do you have any advice?'

'Stock up on tinned peaches,' Bruce says. 'They're on special.'

'No, I mean advice for rescuing Grandpa.'

Bruce fixes me with his spooky jack-o'-lantern stare. 'That *is* my advice. The most evil sorcerer in the Nine Realms suddenly decides he needs the Ruby Ring? It's time to bunker down and wait for the world to end.'

'What?!'

The skull clamps his jaw and the lights in his eyes go out.

Alfie waves his hand in front of Bruce's face. 'Hello? Helloooo? I think he's asleep. Or hibernating, maybe.'

'Well, good,' I say. 'He can hibernate all he wants. There's nothing useful in that guy's head anyway.'

I focus on Grandpa's ring and try a few more times to get a void to open.

Nothing.

Nothing.

Nothing.

'What do we do?' I reach a hand to my tangled hair. Nothing. That odd lock of ice-blue hair is lying flatter than a limp fish. There must be a way to help Grandpa. I mean, he *is* annoying – and obsessed with preparing me to defend the universe against terrible evil – but he's still my grandpa. Or, at least, my great-great-great-grand-something.

And even though Mum and Dad know nothing about being the Protectors or about the Nine Realms or the supposedly oh-so-amazing magical gift Grandpa claims I've inherited, I'm pretty sure they'll blame me if he disappears. Once they notice he's gone, anyway. So that gives us until dinnertime. And speaking of dinner, I'm starving.

'We should probably eat something,' Alfie says, like he's reading my mind. 'I'm all out of samosas, but my nani says food is the gateway to the brain.'

Alfie's nani is the best. She's like this uber-genius quantum physicist who also makes killer snacks. Even thinking about her snacks makes me drool. 'Okay,' I decide. 'First we eat, then you go home.'

'Seriously, Wednesday,' Alfie says. 'I've travelled to another dimension, snorkelled in a lake of slugs, and nicknamed a talking skull. Don't you think it's a bit late for me to just go home?'

I'm too hungry to argue. And secretly, I'm relieved. 'Okay, fine. But no slugs upstairs. Mum'll kill me.'

We raid Grandpa's wardrobe, swapping our sluggy school shorts for velvet pantaloons and trying on every available cloak, hat and robe. Alfie matches a striking pair of purple breeches with some leather moccasins. I go for what might be a hat – or maybe just a sock with a pom-pom on the end – plus an amazing scarf with meteors and planets all over it, and a stripy pair of Grandpa's pantaloons, tucked into a pair of floppy calf-length boots.

I toss my slimy shorts onto Grandpa's laundry pile, remembering to remove the winkleberry just in time. I once washed a red shirt with a bunch of white towels, and let me tell you, that did not go down well. I can't imagine what a magical winkleberry would do. I stick it into the pocket of my pantaloons.

'Okay,' I say to Alfie. 'Sandwich time.'

We pop upstairs and make a few rounds of honey and tahini sandwiches. And Alfie's nani is right. Eating helps.

'Are the other realms all so slimy?' Alfie asks as we make our way back down to the basement.

'Only the Realm of Slugs,' I tell him.

'And there are nine?' he asks. 'Realms, I mean, not slugs.'

'Nine that we know of. There's the Human Realm, the Goblin Realm, the Faery Realm.' I tick them off on my fingers as I go. 'And the Realm of Slugs, of course. Then there's the Realm of Sea Things, the Realm of Unfriendly Cats—'

'There's a realm just for unfriendly cats?' he asks as we reach the bottom stair.

'Sure,' I say, dodging the piles of laundry. 'What other realm would want them? Okay, I think I'm ready.'

Alfie gives me two thumbs-up and his gigawatt grin. Somewhere between escaping sudden death and finishing our sandwiches, he's become part of this adventure, and I'm glad. I can't remember the last time Alfie messed anything up. He could be the perfect antidote to me.

I take a deep breath and sweep the Ruby Ring through the air. '*Open.*'

Nothing happens.

Argh. Grandpa could be slug-bait by now. Or worse.

I gather up all my focus, all my intent.

'*Open!*'

I try again. And again. And again.

Still nothing.

I pull off the ridiculous pom-pom sock-hat and slump onto Grandpa's chair. What's wrong with me? Why won't it work?

Alfie looks for a place to sit, but there's nowhere else – unless you count Grandpa's unmade bed, which smells of sardines on toast and looks like the sheets have been wrestling themselves all night.

In the end, Alfie plonks down on a spare bit of carpet, one of the few spots that's not covered in dirty clothes. Seriously, Grandpa never takes his washing to the laundry. He just drops it on the floor and waits for some kind of Laundry Fairy to magically clean it and return it to his wardrobe.

I stare blankly at the piles of laundry. Maybe old Skully McSkullface is right. Maybe there's nothing to do but sit back and wait for the end of the world. And I don't even like tinned peaches.

No. I'm not giving up.

I jump to my feet, close my eyes, and reach for the magic. It's there, all around me, simmering like a lake of lava. Sometimes it's easy to draw in the amount of magic I need, like when I'm lighting candles or conjuring the Globe of Tarimos.

Sometimes I have to go deeper.

Grandpa says I need to learn control. He says that until I learn control, I have to be careful not to go too deep. But this is an emergency.

Slowly, carefully, I reach for the magic.

Usually, this is the time when things start catching fire or shorting out.

This time it's different.

This time it's like dipping my fingertips into a stream. *Whoa.*

My eyes pop open, and suddenly I'm overflowing with magic. It fills me up like a balloon, then starts fizzing out of me, spinning around the room in wild ripples and eddies. The blue-white lock of hair on my forehead twitches and stirs.

'Wednesday?' Alfie jumps to his feet in alarm. 'Are you all right?'

I ignore him.

Slowly, carefully, I send some of the magic fizzing into Grandpa's ring. The ruby flickers to life, lighting up with a faint red gleam.

It's working!

I pump more magic into the ring, making it glow brighter and brighter.

All the candles suddenly flare like blowtorches, lighting the basement as bright as day. I hear a splashing sound behind me. The dirty dishes in the sink have started washing themselves. A deck of cards shuffles itself and deals out six kings and five aces, while a pair of purple doves spontaneously manifest from a black top hat, fly twice around the room and disappear in a shower of lavender sparkles.

The Ruby Ring glows on my finger like a tiny sun.

This is it. I'm ready.

I swipe my hand through the air and let the magic fly.

'*OPEN!*' I command in a thunderous voice.

The magic pours out of me like a tsunami. I can't control it. Every cupboard in the room crashes open. Every drawer, every box, every bottle and jar. They all burst open, sending their contents flying, and suddenly we're knee-deep in an unholy mess of books, underwear and magical ingredients.

I've opened everything in the room . . . except a portal.

Anger flares inside me, sending sparks bursting through the air like fireworks. I've failed again.

I rip the ring from my finger and hurl it across the room. It tinks off the wall and spins away. I don't hear it land. The candle flames shrink to pinpoints, plunging the room into semi-darkness.

Oh, no. I clap my hands over my mouth and stare after the ring in horror.

What have I done?

Grandpa told me to keep the ring safe, and now I've lost it.

CHAPTER 7

I look around the cluttered basement, trying desperately to spot Grandpa's ring.

'Where'd it go?' Alfie asks.

'I don't know.' I clamber over a mound of recipe books with titles like *101 Ways to Broil Your Dragonwort* and slide down into a drift of unlaundered nightshirts.

'Well, it has to be somewhere,' Alfie says. 'It can't be just gone.'

Fear grips me with icy fingers.

Because here's the thing. Grandpa's ring is the most powerful teleportation device in all the Nine Realms. Being 'just gone' is kind of its thing. Not to mention, powerful magical items like that . . . well, they can be temperamental. And some of them *really* don't like being thrown away.

I swallow hard. 'Help me look.'

After ten minutes of solid effort, we've sifted through enough muddy trousers, knitted scarves and stripy underpants to choke a dragon, but there's nothing. No sign of the ring. It's still buried somewhere in the appalling jumble created by my failed attempt to open the portal. And the fact that the floor was already ankle-deep in Grandpa's dirty washing isn't helping.

I clench my fists in frustration. 'Has he never heard of the laundry?'

As I say the word 'laundry', there's a popping sound and I feel the familiar rippling sensation of a spell being cast. The air around us starts to sparkle.

'What did you do?' Alfie asks nervously.

I shake my head. 'Nothing.'

'Oh, no,' Alfie groans. 'Not again.'

More green sparkles appear, whirling like a tornado made of fireflies. Grandpa's dirty clothes begin to lift off the ground, swirling around and around as they go. I see a glint of red in the pocket of a pinstriped jacket.

The ring!

I lunge to grab it, but I'm too slow.

There's a flash of green light and a puff of lavender-scented smoke. When the smoke clears, all the dirty clothes are gone.

And so is the ring.

Something small and white flutters to the ground.

I pick it up.

It's a small rectangular ticket made of white cardboard, printed with golden letters:

> **LAUNDRY FAIRY DRY CLEANING**
>
> **THE TOWER OF UNBEARABLE BRIGHTNESS (LEVEL 9)**
>
> **THE FAERY REALM**

'So there really *is* a Laundry Fairy,' Alfie breathes.

'Doubt it,' I say. 'Fairies are make-believe. It's faeries you have to watch out for. This is just a marketing gimmick.'

I turn the ticket over. There's more printing on the back:

> **CLAIM TICKET 7066 0820 5547 4493**
> **PLEASE RETAIN THIS TICKET.**
> **NO TICKET, NO CLAIM.**
> **THANK YOU FOR YOUR BUSINESS!**

I stare at the ticket. I've never heard of the Tower of Unbearable Brightness. I've been to the Faery Realm with Grandpa a couple of times, but we always used his ring to get there. And now it's gone.

So . . . the ring was our only chance of saving Grandpa, and I've just sent it to a place that I can't get to without the ring.

I'm the worst apprentice in the history of magic.

'Well done, Apprentice,' a voice says behind me.

I turn.

Bruce the skull is sitting all alone on the now-bare wall of shelves behind Grandpa's workbench. His eyes have lit up and he's grinning at me like ... well, like a skull.

'I didn't think you had it in you,' he says, 'but you've carried out Abraham's wishes perfectly.' His eyelights travel over the cluttered floor. 'I love what you've done with the place, by the way.'

'What are you talking about?' I ask numbly. 'Grandpa told me to keep the ring safe, and now I've lost it.'

'Precisely!' Bruce's teeth clatter with glee. 'You've lost it in the one place the enemy will never be able to find it.'

I shake my head and flop down into Grandpa's armchair. After all that magic, I feel drained, wrung out. I can't think.

Alfie gives Bruce a curious look. 'So who is this Gorgomoth guy, anyway?'

'A very powerful and dangerous sorcerer,' the skull says.

'I kind of got that bit,' Alfie says. 'But, like, any more details? What would his wiki page say?'

Bruce grins. 'He also happens to be King of the Goblin Realm. By the way,' he adds, lowering his voice, 'it's not a good idea to say his name out loud. And whatever you do, don't say it three times.'

'Why not?' Alfie asks.

Bruce ignores the interruption. 'Even his own soldiers call him the Unclean One. And if you'd ever had the misfortune of being trapped with him for a week in a small jungle cave with only jaguar bones and raw truffles for food, you'd know why.'

'Wait,' I say, straightening up. 'You've met him?'

'Naturally. Your grandfather and I went up against him during the Great Goblin War, back in '22. Of course, in those days, he was only a general, but—'

'1922?' Alfie asks incredulously. 'How old are you?'

'*1622.*' The skull cackles. 'And a lot older than I look.' Then his voice turns grim. 'The Great Goblin War lasted fifty years. The losses were terrible on both sides.' Bruce's eyelights flicker, as if he's reliving a painful memory. 'If it wasn't for Wednesday's grandfather, we never would have escaped that cave, and we never would've gone on to win the war.'

Bruce is quiet for a moment. 'Anyway, with the help of Abraham's magic, the Unclean One was defeated and banished back to the Goblin Realm. We thought that was the end of him, but then, a few years back, we started hearing rumours he was gathering a huge army around his fortress.'

'He has a fortress?' Alfie asks from somewhere behind me. 'What's it called?'

55

'The Tower of Shadows,' Bruce says. 'I wouldn't touch that, by the way. It doesn't really like people.'

Uh-oh. I turn to see Alfie reaching into a big old iron-bound chest which I know for a fact has not only been locked and bolted ever since the day Grandpa arrived, but is also protected by a powerful locking spell. Don't ask me how I know.

So I can't help but feel a teensy bit impressed with myself that, thanks to my ludicrously effective attempt at an opening spell, the chest is now gaping wide.

On the other hand, maybe it was locked for a reason.

'What'd you say?' Alfie asks. He straightens up, holding a long sword in a simple black leather sheath.

My stomach does a backflip. 'Alfie, wait!'

Too late. Alfie draws the sword from its scabbard.

CHAPTER 8

As Grandpa's sword slides from its sheath, a strange, cold pulse of magic steals through the room like an autumn frost.

Bruce's eyelights flare, but all he says is, 'Oops.'

'Whoa.' Alfie holds up the sword, admiring the cryptic runes etched into the gleaming steel blade. They're glowing faintly, spelling out a message in some ancient language. 'Check it out.'

'Interesting,' Bruce observes. 'Usually they fall over at this point.'

'Alfie!' I yelp. 'Put it back.'

'No, it's all right,' Bruce says. 'If it didn't like him, he'd be dead already.'

Alfie freezes. 'What?'

Bruce rolls his eyelights. 'I'm joking, obviously.' But

then he winks at me and whispers, 'Like a dodo. Only not as tasty.'

Is he joking? I can't tell. Grandpa's sword always lights up when you touch it. Three years ago, on that fateful meatloaf night, Grandpa was like, 'Touch the sword, Wednesday.' All grave and solemn. So I touched the sword, and it did its lighting-up thing, and then Grandpa did one of his super-annoying mysterious smiles and locked it away, and I never saw it again.

But right now, the old skull definitely seems surprised about something. 'You should be impressed,' he says. 'The Sword of Reckoning does not grant its allegiance lightly. Especially on Tuesdays.'

I frown. I don't know anything about allegiance, but I do know that Grandpa would totally freak if he knew I let Alfie play with his stuff.

'You'd better put it back,' I say, and Alfie reluctantly sheathes the sword and returns it to the chest.

'Anyway,' Bruce says. 'Where were we?'

'Grandpa's ring,' I remind him. 'We have to get it back.'

'Hmm.' Bruce furrows his bony brow. 'Nope, doesn't ring a bell,' he says. 'I'm pretty sure I was telling you about—'

'The Tower of Shadows,' Alfie says, way too enthusiastically.

'Bingo.' Bruce grins. 'The Tower of Shadows, mighty fortress of the goblin kings of old, birthplace of a thousand abominations, twice voted the third-foulest pesthole in all the Nine Realms, et cetera, et cetera, et cetera.'

'Were the previous kings sorcerers too?' Alfie asks.

'What? No.' Bruce clacks his teeth. 'They were just kings. Ruthless, cunning and vindictive for the most part – but that's par for the course with kings, in my experience.' His eyelights gleam. 'Anyway. When we learned that the Unclean One had set up shop in that charming neighbourhood, we knew he had to be cooking up something pretty nasty. He's obviously spent the whole time since the war stealing treasure and magic.'

'Like the Unquenchable Fire?' I shiver, remembering the terrible flames and the stench of sizzling slugs.

'Exactly,' Bruce says gloomily. 'Poor Tariel. I hate to think what the Unclean One did to her to get his hands on that little secret.' He sighs. 'It looks like he's ready to start a new war. All he needs is one last thing.'

Alfie snaps his fingers. 'The ring.'

'Right. Goblins can't travel between realms the way faeries can. So the Unclean One's army is stuck in the Goblin Realm.' He throws a sharp glance at Alfie, who looks like he's about to interrupt again. 'I'm assuming he has no interest in enslaving the Realm of Slugs. But if he gets hold of the Ruby Ring . . .'

'Invasion,' I breathe.

'Yes. Unstoppable goblin armies, sweeping through all the Nine Realms – including this one.'

Alfie gulps. 'He did mention a hot date with enslaving the universe.'

'Which,' Bruce says with a bony grin, 'thanks to Wednesday's quick thinking, has now been averted.'

I frown. Saving the universe is a good thing, right? So why do my guts feel like they've been filled with concrete?

Then it hits me. 'What about Grandpa?'

Bruce's eyelights flicker. 'I'm sorry, Wednesday. There's nothing we can do.'

'What?' I can't believe what I'm hearing. 'No, no, no. We have to rescue him. We have to go to the Faery Realm, find this Laundry Fairy place,' – I brandish the claim ticket – 'get Grandpa's ring back, open the portal, and rescue him.'

'Yeah!' Alfie chimes in. 'And defeat the bad guy, and totally save the world!'

'Right,' I say. 'We can't just leave Grandpa in the Tower of Shadows.'

Bruce's eyelights go dark in a long, slow blink. 'That's what he wanted,' he says at last. His voice is sad. 'That's why he sent you back. Thanks to his sacrifice, the ring is safe. The universe is safe.'

My hands clench into fists and I glare at the skull with such fury it's a wonder he doesn't burst into flames on the spot.

'You mean *you're* safe!' I accuse. 'You want to hide in this basement while Grandpa's tortured by goblins, because you're too afraid to help him.'

'I'm not afraid,' Bruce says in a voice that makes me want to smack him right in his bony mouth. 'I'm merely being logical.'

I prop my hands on my hips and glare at him some more. 'I don't believe you. You're afraid. Afraid of Gorgomoth.'

Bruce's eyelights dart around like fireflies in a jar. 'Would you keep your voice down?'

'Why? What are you afraid of? Do you think Gorgomoth's going to jump out of the cupboard and—'

'Stop saying that name!'

'Gorgomoth, Gorgomoth, Gorgomoth!'

There's a ripple of magic and a sound like breaking glass.

Alfie's eyes go wide as saucers as he stares past me.

Vivid firelight fills the room and the concrete in my stomach turns to ice as I spin around, already knowing what I'm going to see.

The Goblin King is so close I could reach out and touch him. Here in the cramped basement, he's even more terrifying than he was in the swamp. He towers over me, blazing from head to foot with Unquenchable Fire. Through the flames I see his spiky black armour, carved with dozens of screaming skulls and topped off with a huge helmet, complete with a black crown and a giant pair of horns.

All in all, it's quite an entrance.

Gorgomoth the Unclean looks down at me. His red eyes blaze through the skull-shaped faceplate of his helmet, and in a mock-jolly voice he says, 'My ears are burning!'

Alfie screams.

CHAPTER 9

Alfie's still screaming when Gorgomoth raises his hand and manifests his enormous iron battle hammer out of thin air.

'Silence, screaming child!' Gorgomoth booms. At the same time, his whole body flickers on and off like an old TV.

Alfie stops screaming. 'Wait, did you see that?'

I totally did.

'Silence!' Gorgomoth looms over Alfie, his eyes like red-hot coals.

Alfie cringes.

Hmm. There's something fishy going on here. The Goblin King's alight with Unquenchable Fire, but there's no heat. I reach out and swipe at his skull-laden armour, and my hand passes right through his steel-plated knee.

'It's an illusion, right?' I ask Bruce. 'Like a hologram?'

'Right,' Bruce says, but his teeth are still chattering with fear.

'So he can't hurt us?' Alfie asks.

'N-n-not physically,' Bruce stammers. 'But—'

That's enough for me. 'What have you done with him, stinky-bones?'

The Gorgomoth hologram flickers again, then glares down at me. It takes all my courage not to shrink away. 'And just who, or what, are you?' he asks.

Grandpa always says a sorcerer's introduction is her most powerful weapon. And I may not be a sorcerer yet, but I'm the closest thing we've got. I stand up straight, clench my fists, and look the Goblin King square in the helmet.

'I am Wednesday Elizabeth Weeks,' I declare in my best wizarding voice. 'Apprentice of Abraham Mordecai Weeks, Protector of the Realms, Master of the—'

'Yes, yes.' Gorgomoth rolls his fiery eyes. 'I am well aware of the old fool's ridiculous titles.' His entire body flickers on and off again. 'You do realise he makes most of them up.'

Ha! I knew it. But I'm not going to give this big holographic bully the satisfaction of reacting to his taunts. Instead, I just wait. And stare.

'So,' Gorgomoth says when it's clear I'm not going to respond, 'you are his latest pathetic excuse for an apprentice?'

'That's right,' I say, trying to keep the tremble out of my voice. Grandpa's previous apprentices are all hundreds of years before my time, so I don't know much about them. But I know this apprentice, and I know she's furious. 'And, I swear, if you've hurt him—'

Gorgomoth flicks his hand like he's brushing away a fly. 'Spare me your empty threats, miserable apprentice-creature. It is perfectly simple.' He snaps his fingers and an elaborately carved hourglass the size of a barstool appears in his hand. 'If you wish to see your master again, you will bring the Stone of Passage to the Tower of Shadows within twelve of your pitiful human hours.'

He flips the hourglass. Sand the colour of blood starts flowing into the bottom section. 'If not, Abraham Mordecai Weeks will slave without rest in my Pit of Extreme Discomfort for . . .' He pretends to check a non-existent watch. 'Oh, wait. Forever!'

The Goblin King throws back his head and laughs a booming, maniacal laugh that echoes around the basement. Then he clears his throat. 'I'm out of juice. Goodbye.'

There's a puff of toe-jam scented smoke, and the hologram is gone.

Everything's quiet for a long moment, except for a couple of beeping noises as Alfie fiddles with his digital watch.

'That was weird,' Alfie says. Then he sniffs and makes a face. 'Is that toe jam?'

I nod. Because Alfie's right about the toe jam *and* about the weirdness. 'In the swamp he wanted Grandpa's ring, but now he's talking about the Stone of . . .'

All the hairs I never knew I had stand up on the back of my neck.

Alfie looks at me.

'No,' I say, shaking my head. 'It can't be true.'

Surely Grandpa would have told me. On the other hand, it would hardly be the first time he withheld crucial information from me because I 'wasn't ready'.

'What can't be true?' Alfie asks.

I stare at Bruce. 'Tell me it's not true.'

'Sorry, Apprentice.' The skull's eyelights burn with a steady intensity. 'I don't do requests.'

I shake my head. 'You're telling me Grandpa's ring is one of the Seven Stones of Saranon?'

'What's a Saranon?' Alfie asks.

I sigh. Since it looks like Alfie's coming with me on this rescue mission – assuming we can ever get out of this crummy basement – I'd better start filling him in on some facts.

'Saranon was this ancient sorcerer,' I tell him, dredging up a piece of the ancient lore Grandpa's been trying to drill into my head for the last three years.

66

'The *first* sorcerer,' Bruce corrects me. 'Progenitor of all who follow.'

'Okay, okay.' This crotchety old skull is even worse than Grandpa. 'The first sorcerer. Super-powerful. And ten thousand years ago he created these seven magical stones and used them to unite the Nine Realms into a single empire. You know. Mythology.'

Bruce's eyelights flare. 'It is *not* mythology, Apprentice. You, of all people, should know that.'

'Fine.' I shrug. 'Ancient history, then.'

'Seven magical stones,' Alfie breathes. 'That is so cool! It's just like Master Enchanter Zagobar in *Realms of Magic VII.*'

Bruce blinks. 'Zagobar? I know of no such master.'

'He's from a computer game,' Alfie says. 'I'll show you later. So, the Seven Stones?'

'Right.' I go through the list, ticking them off on my fingers. 'The Stone of Power, the Stone of Passage, the Stone of Sight, the Stone of Protection, the Stone of Life, and the Stone of . . . um . . .'

I frown. I can never remember the last one.

'Memory,' Bruce supplies.

I nod. 'Right.'

Alfie looks at me expectantly.

'What?' I ask.

'That's only six,' Alfie points out.

'Huh?' I blink. 'Anyway, now the Stones are lost.'

'Mostly lost,' Bruce corrects.

'Right.' Because, of course, while Grandpa was filling my head with stories about these oh-so-important Stones and their various magical properties, he didn't think it was worth mentioning he was carrying one of them around on his finger. 'And if they fall into the wrong hands it would be, you know, bad.'

'Bad?' Alfie asks nervously.

I nod. 'Like, end-of-the-universe bad.'

'Precisely,' Bruce says in his dry and dusty voice. 'And, as Protector of the Realms, it is Abraham's sworn duty to make sure that doesn't happen. And yours, Apprentice. Which is why you must set aside your feelings and focus on the good of the realms. The Stone of Passage is out of the Unclean One's reach. It must stay that way.'

Huh. Well, Grandpa may have sworn an oath to set his feelings aside, but I never did. And there's no way I'm going to leave a person I care about in a place called the Pit of Extreme Discomfort, no matter what some old skull might have to say about it.

'No.' I fold my arms. 'We're going to rescue Grandpa. And you're going to help us.'

'No.' Bruce sets his jaw. 'I'm not.'

Anger bubbles up inside me again. I can literally feel sparks building up in my fingertips. I want to scream at the skull in frustration. But I don't scream. And I don't incinerate the stubborn old fossil with a blast of magic fire. Which I totally could do if I wanted to. Maybe. Perhaps.

Instead, I take a deep breath, count to five, and ask, 'Why not?'

'Because,' Bruce says, in a voice like a grumpy teacher on a Friday afternoon, 'even if we could retrieve the Ruby Ring – a virtual impossibility in itself, I might add – I happen to know for a fact that the Tower of Shadows is at this moment surrounded by an army of no less than one hundred and seventeen thousand, three hundred and twenty-five goblin soldiers. No, wait.' His eyelights flicker. 'Three hundred and twenty-four. One of them just got killed in a friendly game of—'

'Oh, come on!' I protest. 'Now you're just making stuff up.'

'Making stuff up?' The old skull reacts like I've accused him of kidnapping puppies. 'I most certainly am not!'

Alfie eyes him curiously. 'So how do you know all that stuff?'

'For your information,' Bruce says, 'I happen to be a veritable fount of knowledge, a receptacle of arcane wisdom. I have access to unlimited realms of learning beyond mere mortal comprehension.'

'Really?' Alfie looks impressed.

'Try me.'

I roll my eyes. 'Is this really necessary?'

Alfie ignores me. 'What's the seven hundred and fifty-third prime number?'

'Five thousand, seven hundred and seventeen,' Bruce replies without a second's hesitation. 'You'll have to try harder than that.'

'The atomic number of Caesium?'

'Fifty-five.'

'The secret ingredient in my nani's samosas?'

Bruce's eyelights flicker again. 'Cinnamon.'

'Oh, my gosh!' Alfie turns to me. 'That's totally amazing! He really is a fountain of knowledge.'

'Thank you,' Bruce says primly.

'If you two are quite finished,' I say, 'we only have twelve hours left to rescue Grandpa.'

Alfie checks his digital watch. 'Actually, it's more like eleven hours and forty-seven minutes.' He holds out his wrist so I can see. 'I set a timer. But there's a bigger problem.'

I frown. 'What's that?'

'In four hours and eighteen minutes, I'll be late for dinner, at which point my parents will probably alert the police, the Prime Minister and the entire country.'

'Me too,' I realise. And it's Thai curry night. There's no way I can handle two sets of deadlines. 'I'll leave a note saying I'm having dinner with you tonight,' I tell Alfie. 'You can text your parents to say you're eating with me.'

Alfie looks shocked. He may be an expert at manipu-lating Mrs Glock, but his parents are a whole other matter.

'What?' I ask. 'It's true. Sort of.'

Alfie makes a face like I just told him Pluto's still a planet.

'Look at it this way,' I tell him. 'Would you rather tell them you're off to a parallel dimension to do battle with the most evil sorcerer of the age?'

That seems to help. 'Right. So what do we do about *after* dinner?' Alfie asks.

I shrug. 'We'll have to worry about that later. We just need to buy ourselves a few extra hours. We've got until 2am to rescue Grandpa. And Bruce is going to help us.'

'I told you,' Bruce says testily, 'it's virtually impossible. And it's certainly impractical and illogical.'

'No, it's not.' In fact, it's the opposite of illogical. Because an idea's starting to form in my mind, the faint glimmer of a plan. 'Listen. All we have to do is get to Grandpa. He'll know what to do. I mean, he conquered Gorgo-guy before, right? During the war?'

'Yes, but—'

'Then he can do it again. Look, it'll be easy. All we have to do is go to the Faery Realm, find the ring, then zip over to the Tower of Shadows, grab Grandpa, then zap back home before Gorgo-features knows what's happening.'

I pause for breath, and suddenly it doesn't sound so easy.

'Molten!' Alfie punches the air. 'I am loving this plan. Count me in a hundred and ten per cent!' He frowns. 'But how are we going to get to the Faery Realm without the ring?'

'I don't know,' I admit, but I'm smiling, because this is the best bit. 'But I bet Bruce does.'

CHAPTER 10

Bruce the skull turns his eyelights the other way, like he's pretending not to see me.

'Well, Fountain of Knowledge?' I prompt. 'Anything to say?'

Bruce glares at me. 'I refuse to have any part in—'

'Can you take us to the Faery Realm or not?'

'Not,' Bruce says, sticking out his jaw.

'Hmm.' I try to look him right in the eyelights. 'I feel like there's something you're not telling us.'

He won't meet my eyes.

'Is there something you're not telling us?' I ask.

Bruce clamps his jaw, but the answer escapes his lipless mouth anyway. 'Yes.'

'Oh! I know!' Alfie's eyes light up. 'He can't take us there, but he knows someone who can. I bet that's it.' He looks at Bruce. 'Right?'

Bruce doesn't answer.

'Right, Bruce?' I prompt.

The skull's eyelights roll around in their sockets like marbles and he starts his desperate humming again.

'Or should I call you Maurice?' I ask sweetly. 'Or Dudley? Or Rudolph?'

Bruce's teeth chatter like he's lost in a blizzard.

'Or Skully McSkullface?' Alfie asks.

'All right, fine!' Bruce splutters. 'You're right. There's a way.'

I give Alfie a high-five.

'But I'm telling you,' Bruce says, 'this is not what Abraham wants.'

'I don't care,' I tell him. 'I order you to take us to the Faery Realm.'

'I work for Abraham, not you. You can't tell me what to do.'

'Yes, I can,' I say. 'I'm his apprentice, and you're . . .' I search for something that will get this crusty old skull riled up enough to help save Grandpa. 'You're nothing but a dusty old shelf ornament!'

Alfie gasps.

'Well!' Bruce says, sounding deeply insulted.

'That's right,' I continue. 'And if you don't help me rescue Grandpa, I'll . . . I'll feed you to the neighbour's dog.'

Bruce glares at me. 'You wouldn't dare!'

I glare back. 'Wouldn't I?'

There's an uncomfortable silence. I try to look mean. Our neighbour's dog is a Pomeranian named Fluffy, and she only eats pre-cubed steak, medium-rare. But Bruce doesn't know that. Or does he? Either way, I'm betting he knows enough to realise I won't take no for an answer.

At last the skull lets out a gusty sigh. 'You're even more trouble than the last one. Fine. Pull out my tooth.'

I narrow my eyes. 'Excuse me?'

'Careful,' Alfie warns. 'This one time my cousin asked me to pull his finger, and—'

I wave for Alfie to stop. I'm aware of the finger incident. This sounds more like a request for dental treatment.

'You heard me,' Bruce says.

'Okay,' I say, cautiously. 'Promise not to bite?'

'I'm not a monster,' Bruce says cuttingly. 'It's not like I'd threaten to throw someone to the neighbour's dog.'

Ouch. So maybe that was a bit mean. I resolve to be kinder to Bruce in the future. Carefully, I reach into his mouth and grab hold of a molar. It feels quite firmly attached. 'Are you sure about this?'

''On't 'orry,' Bruce says, through my fingers. 'I 'on't 'eel a 'ing.'

'Okay, then.' I take a deep breath and pull hard. The tooth pops free.

'Aaaaaaah!' Bruce's agonised scream splits the air.

Oh, no! I hold the tooth between my thumb and forefinger, searching for blood.

'I'm so sorry. I—'

'Ha!' Bruce grins. 'Serves you right.'

'Very funny,' I say, still holding the grotty old tooth.

Bruce winks an eyelight at me. The practical joke seems to have cheered him right up. 'Now, slip it under Abraham's pillow.'

I lift Grandpa's pillow, revealing three dead spiders, a handful of peanut shells, and what looks suspiciously like a mummified goldfish.

Gross.

I add Bruce's yellow tooth to the collection and lower the pillow.

'Good,' Bruce says. 'Now, get the sword.'

'The sword?' I frown.

Bruce snorts. 'If you think I'm escorting you two chuckleheads to the Tower of Shadows with nothing for protection but your uncanny ability to open pickle jars, you're sadly mistaken.'

'Oh, fine,' I grumble. 'Anything to get out of here.'

I move towards Grandpa's treasure chest, but Bruce says, 'Not you. The other chucklehead.'

I feel like someone's put a pin in my balloon.

Alfie's face lights up. 'Who, me?'

'Sure,' Bruce says. 'I just need to double-check something.'

Wow. So not only is Alfie better at maths than me, but now—

I take a deep breath. If Alfie takes over sword duties, I guess that's okay. I have enough going on just lighting candles. 'Go ahead.'

Beaming like a class four laser, Alfie retrieves the Sword of Reckoning. Then he spends the next fifteen minutes trying to figure out how to carry it without tripping or cutting off his own feet. Eventually, using a complicated arrangement of belts and buckles, he manages to strap it onto his schoolbag.

'All right,' I say impatiently. 'Now what?'

'Now we wait,' Bruce says.

'For what?' Alfie grins. 'The Tooth Fairy?'

'Obviously,' Bruce replies calmly. 'But don't let her hear you call her that. She's a bit touchy about her new gig.'

'Wait, what?'

'Of course,' Bruce says, regarding me coolly, 'there's still time to reconsider your choices. You wouldn't be the first apprentice to overestimate their own—'

Just then there's a shower of green sparkles. A person with dark, close-cropped hair and filmy gossamer wings appears in the air above Grandpa's bed. She's about my size, but she looks like she spends half her time in the gym and the other half cage-fighting tigers. She's dressed head-to-toe in black – black boots, black combat pants, black tank top. She hovers over Grandpa's pillow, takes Bruce's tooth and slips it into her pocket.

Bruce clears the air that could theoretically be his throat. 'Ahem.'

The Tooth Fairy whirls, whipping a stainless-steel wand from a shoulder holster. I don't even see her move, but suddenly she's hovering right in front of us, her skin golden and her eyes as green as a forest. Her wand is pointed square at Bruce's bony face, its tip glowing with a sullen red light.

'Hey, hey!' Bruce says in a panicky voice. 'Falcon, relax. It's me.'

The Tooth Fairy squints at the skull through titanium-rimmed sunglasses. 'Chuckles?'

Bruce grins. 'In the flesh.'

The Tooth Fairy lowers her wand and runs a hand through her short, spiky hair. 'I didn't recognise you.'

'I know, I know,' Bruce says. 'I've lost weight.'

The Tooth Fairy gives Bruce a deadpan look, then turns her attention to Alfie and me. 'So who are these two?'

'Don't worry about them,' Bruce says carelessly. 'They're with me.'

'Hmm.' The Tooth Fairy looks at me for a moment, then hovers over to stare at Alfie.

'Eep.' Alfie looks like he's swallowed his tongue.

The Tooth Fairy catches sight of the sword strapped to Alfie's schoolbag. 'Wait. Is that . . . ?'

'I'm as surprised as you are,' Bruce says.

'Huh.' The Tooth Fairy takes another long look at Alfie, then shrugs and turns back to Bruce. 'So what's going on, Chuckles? Why'd you call me?'

'I need a favour,' Bruce says. 'We need to get to the Tower of Unbearable Brightness.'

The Tooth Fairy guffaws. 'The Tower? Is this a joke?'

Bruce gives me a pointed look, as if to say, *I told you so*. I give him a pointed look right back, as if to say, *I swear you'll be a dog's breakfast if you don't sort this out right now*.

'Come on, Falcon,' Bruce says. 'You owe me.'

The Tooth Fairy shakes her head. 'That was a long time ago. You can't keep—'

'Reaper's in trouble,' Bruce says quietly.

The Tooth Fairy freezes. Her face turns grim. 'What kind of trouble?'

CHAPTER 11

The green sparkles swirl away, leaving Alfie and me in the middle of a winter forest. I'm carrying Bruce in a sling knotted from Grandpa's meteor scarf. Falcon the Tooth Fairy is hovering next to us, her all-black outfit a stark contrast to the all-white, snow-covered landscape. Even the ancient trees that stand around us are white, so heavily loaded with snow their massive trunks are gnarled and twisted.

At first, I'm pleased I opted for pantaloons and boots. But in seconds, Alfie and I have both sunk knee-deep into the powdery white snow. Fingers of cold creep through the heavy fabric and my breath plumes like smoke in the icy air. I shove my hands into my pockets, feeling the smooth texture of the laundry ticket on one side and the spiky roughness of the winkleberry on the other. Right now I'm wishing we'd thought to bring a couple of Grandpa's cloaks, but my only protection against the cold is my polo shirt.

'Okay, we're here,' Falcon says. She raises her wand. 'Good luck.'

'Hey, wait!' Bruce protests. 'This isn't the Tower. What's going on?'

'Keep your voice down!' Falcon hisses. 'This is the best I can do, okay?' She looks around nervously, like she's expecting something nasty to jump out from behind a tree at any moment. 'I tried to tell you. It's not like the old days. The whole place is . . . well, you'll see.'

I look around. The forest is silent and deserted, nothing but pristine snow and bare trees for miles in every direction.

'Well,' Bruce says, 'could you at least take us to—'

'No.' Falcon shakes her head. 'We're even now. Don't call me again.' She thinks for a moment, then adds, 'And I'm keeping the tooth.'

With a wave of her wand and a burst of green sparkles, she's gone.

'Okay,' I say, doing my best to be cheery despite the fact that Bruce's old army buddy appears to have ditched us in the middle of nowhere. 'We've made it to the Faery Realm. Now what?'

Bruce scowls at me, and I wonder if he's still in a huff about the whole 'feed you to the neighbour's dog' thing.

'Oh, wise and powerful Apprentice,' he says, voice dripping with sarcasm. Yep, definitely still in a huff. 'I would never presume to tell you what to do.'

'Huh, fine.' I roll my eyes. 'Which way to the Tower of Unbearable Brightness?'

'Give me a second.' Bruce's eyelights darken for a moment, then he says, 'It's that way. Two and a half leagues past that ugly old oak tree. The one that looks like your face.'

'Thank you.' Of course, I don't have the faintest clue what a league is, but I'm not going to tell Bruce that. 'Let's go.'

We set off through the snow, past the oak tree that doesn't look anything like my face. It's heavy going. We keep sinking into the snow with every step. Soon we're both huffing and puffing, and my feet are numb with cold.

After about twenty minutes of trudging, a strange wind swirls around us and then dies away.

'Here we go,' Bruce says. 'Hold on to your hats.'

There's a whisper of sound, and suddenly we're surrounded. A dozen heavily armed soldiers have appeared out of thin air. They're all tall and beautiful, and supernaturally clean. Winter faeries. Even in the pale winter sunshine, their intricately carved armour glitters and gleams.

The soldiers glare at us, their eyes so many different shades of piercing blue I feel like I'm in a paint shop. They're all holding spears tipped with sharpened points of pure crystal. And all the spears are pointing straight at us.

'Whoa.' Alfie spins in a circle as he tries to look at all the newcomers at once. 'Who are these guys?'

'Who do you think, numbskull?' Bruce says. 'They're faeries.'

'But I thought faeries were . . . you know.' Alfie makes a vague fluttering motion with his hands.

Instantly, the grim-faced but – I cannot lie – rather good-looking warriors get extra menacing. Unlike their summer cousins, winter faeries don't have wings. I wouldn't exactly say they're sensitive about it, but it's probably not the best ice-breaker, either.

'Watch it,' Bruce warns.

Alfie gulps. 'Obviously, I was mistaken.'

One of the faery warriors steps forward. Instead of a spear, she's armed with a long, curving sword. Her silver armour is studded with diamonds, making her glitter in the pale sunshine like a disco ball. She's clearly their captain.

The faery captain removes her helmet, releasing a cascade of fine, bone-white hair. Her face is pale and supermodel-perfect, with skin like windswept snow and eyes like sapphires.

'Who dares trespass in the dominion of the Winter Queen?' she demands in a voice as cold and forbidding as an arctic glacier.

'Um . . . I'm Wednesday, this is Alfie, and this is, erm, Bruce.' I hold up the skull.

The captain narrows her eyes. 'In the name of Shard the Eternal, Queen of the Faery Realm, I command you to state your business. Speak quickly!'

Alfie steps up beside me and gives her a friendly smile. 'We're on a quest to rescue Wednesday's grandpa from—'

I elbow him sharply in the ribs.

'Ow!' Alfie eyes me reproachfully.

'We're just here about our laundry,' I tell the captain.

'Your companion's sword says otherwise,' she says, glowering at Alfie. Then she reaches out and swipes her fingertip across my cheek.

I'm too surprised to react.

'Hmm.' The captain squints at her finger, clearly unimpressed. She leans down to take a long, hard look at Bruce. 'This one looks familiar.'

Bruce's eyes dart around like a pair of fireflies in a jar. 'Who, me?' he asks. 'Of course I look familiar. I *am* familiar – it's my nature.'

The faery captain narrows her eyes. She's not buying it.

'In fact,' Bruce says, 'some people tell me I'm *over-familiar*. Isn't that right, Shnooky-pumpkin?'

The faery captain recoils, the tips of her pointy ears flushing blue with fury. 'Where did you hear that name?'

Some of the soldiers snicker. It occurs to me that there's a lot more to Bruce than meets the eye. For a disembodied skull, he certainly seems to get around.

'Silence!' the faery captain roars. She points an accusing finger at me. 'You're all obviously goblins in disguise. Spies of the Unclean One.'

'We're not spies,' I protest.

Alfie slinks up beside me, almost exactly like a spy. 'That's right. We're innocent.'

Two of the faery soldiers menace us with their spears.

'That's just what a couple of spies would say,' the first soldier says.

'Yeah.' The second soldier sneers at Alfie's slime-crusted hair. 'They look pretty Unclean to me.'

'Dude, give me a break,' Alfie says. 'I spent half the morning snorkelling in a swamp.'

Okay, this is getting ridiculous.

'I'm telling you, we're not spies.' I pull the claim ticket from my pocket and hold it up. 'We're customers.'

'Let me see that.' The captain plucks the ticket from my hand and eyes it suspiciously. She makes a mystic pass with her hand and the ticket goes all green and sparkly. 'It's real.' She peers at me. 'But this account's not in your name.'

'Of course it's real.' I snatch the ticket back and wave it in the air like a talisman. 'I am Wednesday Elizabeth Weeks, Apprentice of Abraham Mordecai Weeks, Protector of the Realms, Master of the Seven Transformations, Custodian of the Five Ungovernable Charms . . .'

I'm really getting into it, laying on the old Abraham flair by the cauldron-load, but the faeries are clearly unimpressed.

'Honey, you could be Saranon's second-niece for all I care,' the captain says. 'Your name's not in the system.'

'Well, I, um . . .' I stammer to a stop.

Bruce makes another non-existent throat-clearing sound.

I get a horrible sinking sensation in my stomach, like the time I forgot my lines in the school production of *20,000 Leagues Under the Sea*. But then a flash of inspiration hits.

'Maybe not,' I say. 'But I am the authorised representative of a Loyal Customer in Good Standing. And I have . . . a complaint!'

All the soldiers gasp.

'Nice one,' Alfie whispers.

The captain turns pale. 'A complaint?'

From somewhere at the back, one of the soldiers says, 'What do we do, Shnooky-pumpkin?'

'Silence!' the captain roars. 'We shall escort the prisoners to the Tower of Unbearable Brightness. The Department of Claims will decide their fate.'

The soldiers shoulder their spears and form up on either side of us, their blue eyes like lasers. They clearly don't see us as any kind of a threat. They don't even bother confiscating the sword Alfie's wearing strapped to his schoolbag – maybe because it looks like the sword's wearing him.

Oh, well. The important thing is, we're on our way to the Tower of Unbearable Brightness.

'See?' I whisper to Bruce. 'That wasn't so hard.'

The old skull rolls his eyelights and doesn't bother to reply.

CHAPTER 12

Three hours later, after trekking across endless snow and passing through several military checkpoints, all staffed by mean-looking tall-and-trim faery warriors, we finally catch our first sight of the Tower of Unbearable Brightness. I'm exhausted, half-frozen, ready for dinner, and totally sick of listening to Bruce's *I-told-you-so* sighs.

Alfie couldn't be chirpier. 'Eight hours, three minutes left,' he says, checking his watch. 'We are so killing this!'

But it could take at least that long to search this place.

The Tower is super-impressive, a pure-white monolith the size of an office block, topped with a massive sign that says **LAUNDRY FAIRY DRY CLEANERS** in huge glowing blue letters.

'It's a perfect hexagonal prism,' Alfie breathes in wonder.

Soon we're signing our details into a large, leather-bound Visitors Book at reception. It's warm in here – so warm I start to hope I might one day feel my toes again. The air is dry and smells faintly of lavender.

'Everyone needs a badge,' the faery behind the desk intones, holding out a sheet of bright orange **VISITOR** stickers. This faery is dressed all in white, with not a diamond or armoured helmet to be seen. She has green eyes and golden skin. And then, of course, there's the pair of lacy wings. She's a summer faery, like Falcon, only dressed less like a biker, more like a baker.

Alfie and I peel off a sticker each and attach them to our shirts.

'Here,' I say, sticking another one on Bruce's forehead. 'It suits you.' The skull opens his jaw to complain, but I cut him off. 'If you're a good skull, I'll take it off as soon as we rescue Grandpa. Now, let's go.'

A second faery escorts us through a maze of gleaming white hallways, past busy faery workers, all dressed in white, and I'm totally bamboozled by the time we reach the Department of Claims. It's less of a department, more of a desk. The desk is pure white, and next to it is a series of white pigeonholes, all empty. On the desk is a gleaming white in-tray, empty, and an out-tray, also empty. Also gleaming. The entire scene is totally unremarkable, except for the swirling vortex of terror, right behind the desk.

'Check it out,' Alfie says, staring at the vortex.

A single summer faery sits at the desk, dressed in white overalls. He's hard at work when we arrive, rubbing at the top of the empty desk with a fluffy blue cloth.

But all I can think of is the vortex. It's whirling on the back wall like some sort of vertical whirlpool. It's churning and twisting, as if time and space are melting together in a swirling pit of gravitational terror.

I swallow hard and pull myself together. All we need is the ring. Then we're out of here.

'Excuse me,' I say to the faery with the fluffy blue cloth. 'We were wondering—'

The faery holds up a white-gloved hand. 'I'm busy with another customer,' he says. And he returns to polishing the top of his desk.

I look around. There aren't any other customers. I do spot a short, round faery heading our way, pushing a cage trolley stuffed with laundry in all the colours of the rainbow. She's wearing the same standard-issue white overalls, with the added bonus of disposable white overshoes.

'Odd socks,' she says to the polishing faery.

Without looking up, the polishing faery reaches underneath the desk. He must hit some sort of concealed button, because the desk – and the faery with it – swings up to the ceiling like a cat flap.

The other faery wheels her trolley into the space where the desk was seconds before, then moves right up to the swirling vortex on the wall. She opens the cage and starts flinging armful after armful of socks into the whirlpool. As each sock hits the vortex there's a little stainless-steel spark, like static electricity, and the sock is gone.

Alfie gapes. 'Are you seeing this?'

I just nod.

The faery wheels her empty trolley away. The gleaming-white desk swings back down, and the polishing faery continues his polishing, as if nothing has happened.

I try again. 'Erm, excuse me—'

'Busy with another customer,' the polishing faery says, turning his attention to another non-existent spot.

I look across at Alfie, and he nods.

'We have a complaint,' I announce.

The faery snaps to attention. The fluffy blue cloth disappears and he clasps his empty hands on the desk. 'I'm so sorry to hear that,' he says. 'How may I be of assistance?'

Okay, that's more like it. 'Um, yes,' I begin, then launch into my grand introduction. 'I am Wednesday Elizabeth Weeks, Apprentice of Abraham Mordecai Weeks, Protector of the Realms and—'

'Ticket?' the faery says.

'Sorry?'

He reaches into a drawer and plonks a sign on the desk: NO TICKET, NO CLAIM.

'Oh. Right.' I pull the laundry ticket from my pocket and set it on the desk. 'Anyway, my grandfather is—'

The faery raises a hand. 'I'm familiar with your grandfather, Apprentice.' He passes his other hand over the ticket, making it sparkle. Then he nods. 'Now, what is the nature of your complaint?'

I slip the ticket back into my pocket and clear my throat. 'Well, it turns out that a certain . . . item . . . was mixed in with our last batch of laundry.'

The faery sighs and reaches under his desk to retrieve another sign. It reads: WE TAKE NO RESPONSIBILITY FOR LOST ITEMS.

Right.

'It's just that . . . it's not really lost,' I say.

Soon the desk is stacked with yet another sign: PLEASE DON'T ATTEMPT TO CLAIM UNTAGGED VALUABLES, AS REFUSAL MAY OFFEND.

'This is ridiculous. You people took our laundry without asking and now we've lost something really important!'

The faery puts away all his signs and pulls out his fluffy blue cloth. 'First,' he says, 'we didn't take your laundry without asking. No laundry can be removed unless our services are magically requested. Which means *you* asked *us*. And second . . .' He pauses, eyes glittering. 'You're very welcome to look for your item in the Realm of Lost Things. Today's cycle is Daily Wash.' He smiles sweetly through gritted teeth, then gestures behind him to the swirling vortex of terror on the back wall of the office.

Oh great. That's the Realm of Lost Things?

'Now,' the faery says, 'if you don't mind, I need to serve another customer.' He turns back to polishing.

Alfie whoops. 'I have always wanted to travel through space and time,' he says. 'This is going to rock extremely hard.'

'Right.' I nod, trying to find some of Alfie's enthusiasm. 'We jump in, we find the ring, we jump out.' Except, why do I have such a queasy feeling?

There's a strange rattling noise, which is when I remember Bruce. He's been squashed in my meteor scarf sling the whole time. I lift him out so I can look him right in his sockets. 'Bruce, is this vortex safe?'

There's a huge whoosh of air, as if the skull has been holding his breath in his not-actually-there lungs. 'I thought you'd never ask,' he says sarcastically. 'Not that I'm a fount of knowledge or anything. But now that you've *finally* deigned to request information, it is my great pleasure to inform you that if you are foolish enough to enter the Realm of Lost Things, you will never get out. It's a one-way system. Once lost, items of laundry are never recovered. This is a basic rule of the universe, and your odds of discovering the ring if you do enter the vortex are approximately one in three million, four hundred thousand and twelve, which means that, frankly, even thinking about going in there is a ridiculous and illogical idea that no one in their right mind would ever condescend to call a plan.'

I get the feeling he's been saving that speech for a long time.

Suddenly I feel warm towards the old bone. I know he has my best interests at heart, or at skull, or whatever. And it's looking less and less possible that we'll be able to pull off this rescue idea. He's been totally right about almost everything so far.

'Thanks, Bruce!' I hold him up and kiss him, right on his orange **VISITOR** sticker. Then I hand him to Alfie.

'Take care of each other,' I say, trying not to think about how I'll feel when the two of them are gone. 'And don't forget to sign out at reception when you leave.'

I turn to the polishing faery. 'Excuse me, but I have business in the Realm of Lost Things.'

'Wait, wait, wait,' Alfie says. 'You're not going without me, right? Like I said, journey through space and time! Plus, I really dig your grandpa. I'm all for this rescue, even though the odds, mathematically speaking, aren't great.' He grins at me. 'Magically speaking, though, I think we're in good hands.'

I look at him.

'Your hands, Wednesday,' he says. 'Besides, we're a team.'

I feel a warm glow in my guts. It feels good to be part of a team.

'What about Bruce?'

'We could ask this guy to look after him.' Alfie points to the faery, who is suddenly polishing with renewed vigour. 'He could probably do with a shine-up.'

Bruce makes a choking noise.

'Something you'd like to say?' I ask.

'Oh, for goodness sake,' the skull huffs. 'If you're so set on this ridiculous "plan", then you may as well take me with you. There's no way I want to spend the rest of my life as a hair stand for the Department of Washed Wiggery.'

The glow spreads to my heart as I tap on the faery's super-clean desk. 'Excuse me, can you let us through?'

The faery ignores me.

'Please?'

Nothing.

Then Alfie steps in. 'Odd socks,' he says with a grin.

The faery rolls his eyes, hits the button, and he and the desk swing up to the ceiling. The way to the vortex is clear.

We step right up to the swirling madness. A warm wind ruffles my hair. It smells like lavender and ocean breeze and almost-certain death.

My knees are knocking, which is super-uncomfortable when you're wearing pantaloons, but I think of Grandpa's face and it gives me courage.

'Here goes nothing,' I say, and jump in.

CHAPTER 13

Darkness.

More darkness.

Endless spinning, random pauses, spinning some more. I'm inside the vortex for what seems like hours. The spinning makes me drowsy. I try to fight it, but now the air is full of some kind of sweet perfume, and my eyelids are getting heavy, and . . .

Aaah! I claw my way out of a smothering dream involving evil clowns and a giant cement mixer full of fairy floss. The spinning has stopped – thank goodness – and I'm lying on something soft, but it's still dark. I mean, it's as dark as the inside of a dragon.

I'm not panicking, though. Not even close.

I take a long, deep breath, just to prove how calm I am. The air is warm and dry, but kind of . . . thin. Like every molecule's been inhaled and exhaled a million times. And it's quiet. Like, imagine you're standing a mile underground on a dead planet, deep in the infinite void of space. That's how quiet it is.

'Hello?' I say.

Nothing.

'Alfie? Bruce?'

Still nothing.

Okay, *now* I'm starting to panic. My heart jerks into double time and I start sucking quick, shallow breaths. And then something touches my face and for some reason it makes me think of giant spiders and I just *lose it*.

'*Light!*' I scream.

With a faint ripple of magic and a shower of staticky sparks, the Luminating Globe of Lost Tarimos manifests in front of my face. I've never been so happy to see anything in my whole life. Because finally I can see where I am, and it's . . .

Good grief.

It's a wardrobe.

White melamine walls rise on either side of me like office towers, their tops lost in the gloom beyond the reach of the light spell's pale glow. Each wall is studded with thousands of shiny chrome hooks, and every hook is hung with an item of clothing.

There are T-shirts and polo shirts. There are tank tops and turtlenecks. There are jumpers, jackets, pullovers and parkas. There are trousers, track pants, blue jeans and bloomers. There are underpants of every conceivable size, colour and design. And on the floor, socks. Nothing but socks, from one wall to the other. And no two of them are alike.

Wow. And I thought *Grandpa's* wardrobe was messy.

A red-and-green tartan scarf with tassels on the end settles silently back against the wall in the faint stir of an invisible breeze.

That must be what touched my face. I let out a sigh of relief. Giant spiders, indeed.

I touch my own scarf, the one with meteors on it, and with a start I realise it's dry. In fact, my whole outfit is dry. And clean. No more slug gunk or snow grime. And I can feel my toes again too, the bone-chilling cold of the snow-covered Faery Realm now just an unpleasant memory.

But where am I?

The towering walls stretch away in both directions, forming a narrow corridor as far as the light can reach. The whole place feels . . . forgotten. Abandoned.

Lost.

Well, I may be lost, but I don't plan on staying that way. I need to find the ring. And rescue Grandpa. But first I need to find my friends – plural, if you count the talking skull. And that means I need to get moving.

I pick a direction at random and set off along the corridor, but right away there's a problem. The Globe of Tarimos stays put, hovering in mid-air like a lamp without a lamp post, leaving me walking into darkness.

'Um, *heel*?' I say. I've only ever conjured the globe in one place, but there's no way I'm exploring this wardrobe in the dark. I try walking away again, but the globe stays exactly where it is. Great.

I close my eyes again, picture myself, then picture the globe. I picture it following me. '*Heel*,' I tell it, then open my eyes.

This time, when I walk away, the globe follows like an obedient puppy, hovering over my head, making my shadow loom and bounce along the path in front of me.

Awesome. I continue along the corridor, pushing through the clutter of hanging clothes. Headless hoods and limbless arms reach for me as I squeeze past. Silk scarves flutter, but there's no noise, no sign of life.

Then the corridor splits into three. A crossroads.

I take a deep breath and go left.

Another crossroads. Then another. And that's when I realise.

This is no ordinary wardrobe. It's a maze.

Well, I've solved mazes before. Mostly on paper, never in a closet. But how hard can it be?

I walk left. Then right. Then left again. Then maybe . . . right?

I'm starting to understand how children can get lost in wardrobes.

And then I remember the maze from school, and Mrs Glock standing in front of her whiteboard. 'Program your robot to follow one wall,' she said, her red pen turning left at every crossroads. 'And follow . . . and follow . . . until it reaches . . . the end!' Her red pen triumphantly exited the whiteboard maze. 'Now,' she said. 'It's your turn.'

Okay, Mrs Glock. I just hope I don't explode.

I start walking, sticking to the left-hand wall at every turn. When I get to a dead-end, I don't panic. I simply turn and continue walking along the left-hand wall.

Keep left. Keep left. Keep left.

I walk for what feels like hours. At first all I can hear is my own footsteps and steady breathing – but soon I can hear odd rustling and slithering noises, like something's tracking me through the maze. I whirl and stare into the darkness, but there's nothing.

So I keep walking.

Keep left. Keep left. Keep left.

I'm concentrating so hard, I don't notice the sound until it's almost on top of me.

It's a voice.

A low, sad voice.

'Five thousand, seven hundred and forty-three,' the voice says. 'Five thousand, seven hundred and forty-nine.'

It sounds like somebody's reciting prime numbers.

'Five thousand, seven hundred and . . . um . . .' the voice falters. 'Seventy-nine? Yes. Five thousand, seven hundred and—'

My heart skips a beat. Because there's only one person I know who loves prime numbers enough to recite them while they're lost and alone in the dark, and that's—

'Alfie?'

The voice stops. 'Wednesday?'

It *is* Alfie!

And he's close. I race around the next corner, expecting him to be right there, but there's nothing. Just another endless, laundry-lined corridor.

I look around, confused. 'Alfie?'

'Up here.' His voice drifts down from somewhere high above.

I look up and there he is, hanging from a hook like an item of discarded laundry. He's so high up I can barely see him in the gloom.

'Thank goodness you're here,' he calls down. 'I was nearly out of prime numbers.'

I frown. 'What?'

'That was a joke.' He pauses. 'You know, because of Euclid's theorem?' He clears his throat. 'Anyway, now that you're here, maybe you can . . .' He makes a mystic gesture. 'You know, magic me down? I'm kind of stuck.'

Apparently, despite the disaster in Grandpa's basement, Alfie somehow thinks I'm some kind of amazing, fully fledged sorcerer. But the sad fact is, although I do know a levitation spell, I've never actually levitated anything bigger than a pencil.

So magic's out, but that doesn't mean I can't help. I'll just have to do it the old-fashioned way. I reach up, grab a couple of hooks, and hoist myself onto the wall.

I start climbing, and it's easier than I expected. The evenly spaced hooks make perfect hand- and footholds, and the Globe of Tarimos rides along with me, hovering over my shoulder like my own personal booklight. In a couple of minutes I'm there, clinging to the wall next to Alfie, puffing and panting in the thin, dry air.

'Hey,' I say.

Alfie gives me his biggest smile. 'Hey.'

'Any sign of Bruce?' I ask, helping Alfie wriggle free of his hook.

Alfie shrugs. 'Not even an eye roll.'

We call Bruce's name a couple of times, but there's no reply – just the stifling silence of the maze.

Alfie collects his backpack, sword still attached, from a neighbouring hook. 'What is this place?'

'Some sort of maze. I've been walking for hours with no sign of—'

'Not hours,' Alfie says, checking his watch. 'There's six hours and forty-eight minutes left on the clock. Which means it's only been . . . seventy-five minutes since we arrived at the Tower, if we're being precise.' He looks at me quizzically. 'Do you think Gorgomoth is the kind of evil overlord who likes to be precise?' Then his eyes light up. 'Wait, did you say *maze*?'

After that, Alfie insists we climb the rest of the way to the top. When we get there, I pop my head up and look around. In the faint circle of light cast by the Globe of Tarimos I can see the tops of about ten more walls, all arranged in the random maze-pattern I've become so familiar with down at ground level. Beyond that, everything fades into darkness.

'Can you make it brighter?' Alfie asks.

I frown. It's a good question. Can I? As far as I know, the Luminating Globe of Lost Tarimos only has two settings – dim and dimmer. On the other hand, before today I didn't know it could follow me around, either.

I close my eyes and concentrate, drawing in a little magical power. Then I pump the power into the Globe of Tarimos and say, '*Brighten.*'

There's a faint ripple of magic and the globe blazes up like a tiny white sun.

Alfie turns his face away, squinting against the glare. 'Okay, now I *really* can't see.'

But I'm not done yet. I draw in a little more magic and pump it into the globe. '*Rise.*'

And, just like that, as neat as you like, the globe starts to rise, getting brighter and brighter as I pump more magic into it, spreading its light further and further across the maze.

Alfie's eyes widen. 'Whoa.'

Okay, *now* we can see. And it's good news and bad news. The good news is, by controlling the Globe of Tarimos like that, I feel like I've made a minor magical breakthrough. The bad news is . . .

Well. The bad news is, the maze is *huge*.

CHAPTER 14

The Globe of Tarimos cuts through the gloom and I stare, open-mouthed, at the gigantic maze that stretches to the horizon in every direction. At first, I think we must be at the bottom of a valley, because I can see the ground rising in the distance, like a gently rolling maze-covered hillside. But then my eyes reach the horizon – or where the horizon ought to be – and I realise there *is* no horizon. There's just more maze.

So I look higher, and higher, and then higher still, until I'm staring straight up at the sky. But there *is* no sky. There's just more maze.

And suddenly it's like the whole world has turned upside down, and now I'm a mile in the air, hanging by my feet from a couple of flimsy hooks and looking down from a birds-eye view at a tiny maze far, far below.

I squeeze my eyes shut and grab Alfie's arm. 'Make it stop!'

'I know, right?' Alfie's voice is full of wonder. 'This place is off the sprocket!'

And I have to agree – if by 'off the sprocket' Alfie means 'a grotesque violation of all known laws of physics and sanity'.

Why? Why? Why?

Why would someone go to all the trouble of building a spatially and gravitationally impossible wardrobe-maze on the inside of a colossal sphere, and then just fill it with random items of laundry? It doesn't make any sense.

I carefully open my eyes, keeping them fixed on a nice red-and-white polka-dotted sock down there on the ground – the real ground, thirty metres below my feet – not that other fake, treacherous ground a thousand metres or so over my head. I start climbing down, focussing all my energies on making it safely back to that sock.

Alfie starts down after me. 'What did that faery dude say this place was called again?'

I grit my teeth and silently swear a vow of terrible vengeance against the smug faery from the Department of Claims. 'The Realm of Lost Things.'

'The Realm of Lost Things,' Alfie breathes.

We've finally reached the ground, so I feel brave

enough to take my eyes off the sock and look at Alfie's face. His eyes are popping with admiration and wonder.

'Is this another one of the Nine Realms?' he asks. 'It seems a bit cramped.'

I shake my head. 'No. This place is something else. It's like some kind of weird pocket dimension.'

'Molten!' Alfie says. 'No wonder Bruce said we'd never get out.'

Speaking of Bruce, where is that know-it-all skull? I hope he's not stuck in a sock or something. If he is, we'll never find him.

I'm so busy thinking about Bruce it takes a few seconds for Alfie's words to sink in. 'Wait, what? Of course we'll get out. It's only a maze, right? We can use the wall-following algorithm, like in robotics class, and—'

Alfie shakes his head mournfully, then offers me a drink from his water bottle.

'Why not?' I ask, taking a swig. Apart from a few minor details, like inside-out gravity or whatever it is that makes this place tick, the actual maze layout looks pretty standard.

'Well,' Alfie says, 'according to my calculations, the average solution distance for a square maze N metres across is N-squared over two!'

Obviously, my maths isn't as good as I thought it was, because I honestly don't see the problem. I mean, I know there must *be* a problem, because Alfie's looking at me like he just told me my new puppy was run over by an ice-cream truck.

'Okay,' I say, handing the bottle back. 'So?'

Alfie takes a sip, then tilts his head and gives me a look.

Okay, I know that look. It's a look that says, *How do you expect to learn anything if I just tell you the answers?* And he's got a point. But we now have somewhere less than seven hours to save Grandpa – so I glare at Alfie and give *him* a look that says, *Kindly go suck a lemon and just tell me, already.*

Alfie sighs. 'So, for a square maze ten metres across, we'd have to walk an average of fifty metres to get out. Pretty easy, right? For a hundred-metre maze, the average distance would be five thousand metres.'

'Okay,' I say slowly. I'm starting to see where he's going with this. But I'm still not sure how his formula translates to our current situation. Without looking up, I gesture at the upside-down maze dome arching impossibly overhead. 'So what's the formula for a freaky inside-out insanity maze?'

He gives me the look again, but I already have the beginnings of an idea, so I say, 'Wait. We're inside a sphere, right? And the formula for the surface area of a sphere is . . . um . . .' I search my brain, and amazingly, the answer comes to me. '$4\pi r^2$.' Thank you, Mrs Glock.

Alfie grins. 'Nice.'

'So if the sphere is, what, a thousand metres across?'

'Easily,' Alfie agrees.

'Okay. Then the radius would be five hundred metres. Which means we'd have to walk . . .'

I scrunch up my face while I work on squaring 500, then multiplying by 4 and by 3.14, and dividing the whole thing by 2.

'Fifteen hundred and seventy thousand metres,' Alfie says helpfully.

Wow. He did that in his head.

'So that's what? Fifteen kilometres?' It's worse than I thought, but it's not too bad. 'If we run, we can—'

'Wednesday,' Alfie says, and now I *know* my maths isn't as good as I thought it was, because he's giving me the flat-puppy look again. 'It's not fifteen kilometres. It's fifteen *hundred* kilometres.'

Ah, nuts.

When I've recovered from the shock, I try to look on the bright side. 'But that's only the average, right? We could get lucky.'

But even I know I'm clutching at straws with that one. When whoever built this place was filling out design forms with their mad architect, I highly doubt they would have ticked the box marked 'easily escapable by luck alone'.

For a moment I want to lie down, make myself comfy on a really thick pile of socks, and go back to sleep. But then I think about Grandpa spending the rest of his life slaving in Gorgomoth's Pit of Extreme Discomfort when the sand runs out of that hourglass.

So I straighten my back and say, 'Well, we've got to try. What else can we do?'

Alfie's eyes brighten. 'Let's cut our way out.'

He reaches over his shoulder and grasps the hilt of Grandpa's sword. The three-foot blade glides from its sheath with a deadly whisper of steel – or at least, that's what *would* have happened if Alfie's arm was long enough. Instead, the blade gets stuck halfway, slightly spoiling the effect. But, after a few seconds of hopping and some awkward-looking contortions, Alfie manages to draw the sword. Clutching the hilt with both hands, he brandishes the gleaming blade over his head, then charges forward with a fierce battle cry and attacks the nearest wall.

'Ha! Ha! Heeyah!' He hacks at the wall with terrifying enthusiasm.

Okay, I don't know much about melamine, but if the countertops in our kitchen are anything to go by, I'm pretty sure you can scratch the stuff just by looking at it. Certainly, I would have thought the Sword of Reckoning would at least be able to get through the veneer.

But no matter how hard Alfie slashes and hacks, the sword simply bounces off without leaving a mark. Maybe whoever built this place decided to splash out and give their giant wardrobe a magical sword-proof coating. Or maybe there's a simpler explanation. Maybe Grandpa's sword hasn't seen a sharpening stone since 1622.

Puffing and panting, Alfie lowers the sword. 'A little help?'

I look at the sword and shrug. 'I don't think it's sharp enough.'

'I don't mean the sword,' Alfie says. 'I'm talking magic, baby! Can't you just . . . I don't know. Shatter it into atoms with a blast of mystic fire?'

I frown. 'Mystic fire?'

'Sure, you know. Like, RAAAAH!' Alfie strikes a wizarding pose and raises his hand towards the wall, fingers extended like claws. 'MYSTIC FIRE!'

'Sorry.' I shake my head. 'I don't think I know any mystic fire spells.'

'Oh, go on,' Alfie urges. 'What about that one your grandpa did in the swamp? I bet that could blast through anything.'

Hmm. I think back to the bolt of magical energy Grandpa hurled at Gorgomoth back in the Realm of Slugs. Even though he dressed it up with a bunch of fancy incantations, I'm pretty sure that particular spell is about as simple as it gets – you just suck in as much magical force as you can hold, then fling it at whatever you want to explode.

It's all about raw power, which is something I've never had a problem with. Normally I have to bend over backwards so things *don't* explode. It might be nice to blow something up on purpose for a change.

Besides, I just taught the Globe of Tarimos to heel, and brighten, and rise. Maybe Grandpa's right. Maybe I do have what it takes to be the next Protector of the Realms.

'All right,' I say. 'I'll give it a go.'

'Yeah, baby!' Alfie dances up and down with excitement. 'This is gonna be succulent!'

'You'd better stand back,' I tell him.

He sheathes Grandpa's sword and retreats about twenty metres down the corridor, then gives me a wave and a double thumbs-up.

Feeling slightly ridiculous, I close my eyes, take a deep breath, and open my senses. The magic's there, all around me, hot and fiery. I reach out and let it boil into me, but this time I keep it locked down tight. I draw in more and more power, squeezing tighter and tighter until it's blazing inside me like a supernova.

Then I brace my feet, point my palm at the wall and say the first word that pops into my head. *'Boom.'*

With a blinding flash, a blast of pure energy erupts from my hand. It rockets through the air and slams into the wall like a thunderbolt.

Then it bounces straight back and blows me off my feet.

CHAPTER 15

The magical blowback from my failed attempt at maze remodelling throws me ten metres down the corridor. I land on my back and skid another four or five metres, ploughing up a mound of socks the size of a small car.

Well, that didn't work.

When I can breathe again, the first thing I do is make sure my arms and legs are still attached. Actually, that's the second thing. The first thing I do is check my hair. It's still there – thank goodness – and it's not even on fire, although it feels like it's been frizzed to within an inch of its life. Except for the blue streak, of course. That still feels smooth and strong.

In good news, I clearly hit the magical jackpot, so let's call that a win. In bad news, the wall's still standing, its surface as smooth and unblemished as ever.

'Wednesday! Are you all right?' Alfie races up and helps me to my feet.

I brush myself off. 'I'm fine.'

Alfie's almost dancing with excitement. 'That was totally molten! I mean, the wall didn't shatter into atoms or anything, but—'

He claps his hand to his mouth and stares at me, wide-eyed.

'What?' I ask crossly. 'What is it? Have I got something on my face?'

'On your face?' Alfie gulps. 'Um . . . no?'

Oh, no. My stomach shrinks like a week-old balloon. Not again.

I reach up and touch my forehead, right above my eyes.

There's nothing. Nothing but a terrible smoothness.

My eyebrows are gone.

My jaw clamps tight and my fists clench. 'Oh, well that's just *GREAT.*'

Alfie shrinks back. 'You're not mad at me, are you?' He peers at my face in confusion. 'Seriously, are you? I can't tell.'

I throw him a glare of such ferocious intensity it's a wonder he doesn't burst into flames on the spot. In fact—

Uh-oh.

Alfie's hair starts to smoke.

'What's that smell?' he asks. Then his eyes bug out and he screams, flapping frantically at his hair.

Ah, nuts. Not again.

I lunge forward, grab the bottle from the side pocket of his backpack and dump water over his head.

The fire goes out with a sizzling splash.

'Are you okay?' I ask.

Alfie stares at me, his face a mixture of hurt and disbelief. 'You set my hair on fire!'

'It was an accident, I swear.' I reach for the frizzled, soggy mess on top of his head. 'Here, let me—'

Alfie pushes my hand away. 'It's fine, all right? I'm fine. Let's just go.'

'But . . .'

'I said it's fine.' Alfie stomps off, a sure sign that everything's about as far from fine as it can be.

I trail miserably behind him, and we navigate the maze in silence for a while. We trace the left-hand wall through every cul-de-sac, blind alley and dead end until our feet are blistered and our lungs are burning in the hot, dead air. I shuck my meteor scarf, and shove it into my pocket – the one with the laundry ticket, not the one with the winkleberry. The last thing I need is a stupid winkleberry snagged in my favourite scarf.

As we walk, my mood grows blacker. Alfie's still mad about his hair, and I feel terrible about what happened, but I don't know how to make it right. On top of that, my eyebrows are singed off, Bruce is still missing, my stomach is grumbling, and we have less than six hours before the sand runs out of Gorgomoth's hourglass. It feels like we're further than ever from escaping this stupid maze.

We walk on. The clothes cluster more thickly on the walls, multiplying like coloured fungi. Now each hook has nine or ten items hanging from it instead of only one. The socks grow deeper underfoot and the dangling clothes close in overhead until we're picking our way through a dark, suffocating tunnel of laundry.

The Globe of Tarimos hovers lower and lower, sticking close as I duck and weave between the bulging walls of fabric. I do my best to avoid touching anything for fear of causing a wave of lost and angry laundry items to tumble from their hooks in a suffocating landslide.

Suddenly Alfie stops dead. 'Oh, my gosh! I don't believe it.'

'What?'

He points to a navy-blue bucket hat perching on a crowded hook just above eye level. 'That's my hat. I lost it at the Year Three sports carnival.'

No way. 'Are you sure?'

Alfie frowns. 'Of course I'm sure. It's got my Atomic Energy merit badge on it. See?'

I peer up at the hat. There is indeed a bright yellow merit badge stitched to the front of it.

Alfie reaches up. 'I love that hat.'

'Wait!' I say. Too late.

Alfie grabs the hat and crams it happily over his scorched hair. In the process, he dislodges a long silk scarf that slithers off the hook and slides silently to the floor. As it falls, the scarf brushes a purple top hat. The top hat wobbles, then tumbles down, dislodging a pair of red-and-white striped trousers. And a feathered tutu. And a black bathrobe. Suddenly the entire bulging contents of the wardrobe are tumbling from the walls. A laundry tsunami!

I grab Alfie's hand. 'Run!'

We run. The walls close in behind us, a chain reaction of lost scarves and jackets, robes and hats . . .

I'm towing Alfie behind me, pelting as fast as I can through the carpet of socks.

The rushing wind of collapsing fabric whooshes at our heels.

I pump my legs, haul Alfie along beside me.

There's an intersection in front of us, but it's too far ahead. We're not going to make it.

Something snags my ankle, like a belt or maybe a live snake. I try to kick it off, but it clings tight.

Alfie grabs my arm and drags me forward.

The intersection gets closer. Closer.

Now! I roll left and Alfie dives to the ground beside me. The avalanche continues straight down the hall.

We're safe.

Alfie sits up and brushes himself off. Then he reaches up to touch his head. 'Oh!' he groans. 'My hat!'

Without the hat, Alfie's half-charred hair is on full display. I try not to look. Try not to feel guilty. I mean, whose idea was it to blow up the wall in the first place?

We keep walking, and the only thing that distracts me from Alfie's hair is the distinct and growing feeling that something's following us.

At the next intersection, something rustles in the darkness on our right.

'Let's go left,' Alfie says nervously.

So we do. I try not to think about giant spiders.

At the next turn, I swear I can hear the clacking of teeth, somewhere in the distance down the left-hand corridor.

'Let's go right,' I decide.

Finally, our corridor empties into a giant square cavern, about the size of a basketball stadium. White melamine walls tower on all four sides, unblemished by hooks or laundry. The air is warmer than ever, crackling with static electricity and thick with a hot, dry laundry smell.

There's only one way in – the corridor we just left. And one way out – an identical hook-lined corridor on the far side of the clearing. The ground between is covered in some kind of smooth, bluish-grey carpet.

I step onto the carpet and instantly sink up to my knees. 'What the—?'

I look down. It's not a carpet at all. It's a thick, dry layer of fluffy grey fuzz.

Alfie scoops up a handful of the stuff. He rubs it between his fingers and gives it a cautious sniff. 'I think it's lint.'

I frown. 'Lint?'

'Sure, like in a clothes dryer.' He looks around in disapproval. 'You know, they really should clean this out. A dirty lint trap can be a real fire hazard.'

'Fire hazard?' I ask, staring nervously at the giant pond of highly flammable cotton-and-nylon fuzz in which we're now standing.

'Yeah,' Alfie says, touching his ruined hair. 'I guess I better watch what I say, huh?'

Ouch. I feel another pang of guilt. 'Alfie . . .'

'Come on,' he says, turning away. 'I'll go first.'

We wade out into the lint trap. A sea of fluff closes silently behind us, getting thicker and deeper as we move forward. By the time we reach the middle it's up to my waist, and I'm praying it doesn't get any deeper.

Suddenly Alfie freezes. 'Um, Wednesday? Is there something alive in here?'

I flash back to the imaginary rustling noises that definitely weren't stalking us through the maze, and suddenly something about the word 'trap' just doesn't feel right.

'Out of curiosity,' I say, much too casually, 'why do you ask?'

But I never get to hear the answer, because that's the moment when something grabs Alfie and yanks him under the surface.

His scream is swallowed by the lint.

Alfie's gone.

CHAPTER 16

'Alfie!' I scream, lunging for the spot where he disappeared.

There's no sign of him.

'Alfie!'

Suddenly it doesn't matter whose fault it was that Alfie's hair got singed. It doesn't matter that I'll never be a good apprentice. All that matters is Alfie. I dive forward, flailing desperately through the fuzz.

Then the lint boils with movement, and Alfie pops up like a cork with a bad case of dandruff, his arms and legs flailing and snowflakes of lint exploding off him like cottony fireworks. He's still wearing his backpack, but there's something else wrapped around his neck. Something long and thin and . . .

I blink.

Okay, it's definitely a red-and-green tartan scarf with tassels on the end.

But this is no ordinary scarf. It *moves* with horrible purpose, writhing and twisting around Alfie's throat, drawing tighter with every panicked breath.

'Help!' Alfie yells, struggling to keep his head above the lint.

I dive forward and grab his foot and suddenly the scarf-monster and I are engaged in a horrible tug-of-war, with Alfie as the rope. And now he's choking, and reaching over his shoulder, but the scarf-tentacle throws a coil over his desperately flailing arm.

'The sword!' Alfie gasps.

Of course! I lunge for Alfie's schoolbag.

The instant I let go of Alfie's foot, the scarf-monster whips him high into the air and now he's thrashing and flailing and raining lint, two metres over my head.

But Grandpa's sword is in my hand. A surge of magical power tingles up my arm and – I'm not even kidding – the entire blade lights up with an ice-cold, luminous-green glow.

Whoa! It's never done that before.

I step forward and aim an awkward swipe at the scarf-monster. With a silken whisper, the Sword of Reckoning slices through the writhing tentacle like it's not even there.

Okay, then. I guess it wasn't blunt after all.

With a high-pitched keening sound, the severed scarf-tentacle whips out of sight. Alfie drops like a stone, disappearing into the fluff.

I reach in and haul him to his feet. 'Are you all right?'

He coughs out a cloud of lint and gives me a shaky thumbs-up.

But then a tremor shakes the ground and a low, horrible groan fills the air. The lint churns into a seething whirlpool as something rises from the deep.

Something big.

Alfie staggers back. I stare in horror at the *thing* that's slowly rising into view, and now I'm wishing for giant spiders. Because the nightmare taking shape in front of us is much, much worse. It's . . . well . . .

This one time, Grandpa took me to the Realm of Sea Things, looking for mermaid scales in the ruins of Drowned Atlantis, and we had a run-in with a kraken. Which is basically a ravening, flesh-eating octopus the size of a school bus. You don't want one of those things lurking at the bottom of your swimming pool, believe me.

And the monster rising from the lint is just like that. Except the whole thing is made up of thousands of bits of discarded laundry. And it totally missed the memo about only having eight arms.

'It's a kraken!' I shout, as dozens of tentacles emerge from the lint and soar into the air, writhing like a nest of snakes. Each tentacle is made from a pulsing web of lost clothing. 'A laundry kraken!'

Alfie frowns. 'What's a *kracken*?'

I slash at a flailing tentacle with Grandpa's sword. 'You know. A kind of giant octopus thing.'

Another tentacle lunges at Alfie. He skips out of reach and says, 'Oh, you mean a *krahken*. It's from the Norwegian, you know.'

I roll my eyes, but secretly I'm glad to have my brilliant friend back. '*Kracken, krahken*. Whatever!' I hack away another tentacle, and the monster roars in fury. 'It's a giant squid made of laundry, okay?'

'Okay, okay. But the Norwegian . . .' Alfie breaks off, staring at the beast in surprise. 'Hey! Is that my hat?'

I look where he's pointing.

And, yes. The laundry kraken is indeed wearing Alfie's hat.

But only for a moment. It's soon sucked into the churning, boiling mess of robes and scarves and trousers that is the monster. Because the kraken is forming and re-forming itself before our eyes, the largest laundry pile in the world, come to ravenous, terrifying life.

A forest of tentacles rises in front of me, dodging and weaving, just out of reach of the sword. More tentacles close in on Alfie, menacing him from all sides.

'Um, Wednesday?' he calls. 'A little help?'

I charge forward and hack at the tentacles, but the monster has grown wary of the flashing blade, and I'm too slow to land a single blow. A tentacle whips around Alfie's leg and another snags his arm. I hack and slash, but I can't reach him.

The tentacles drag Alfie to his knees. In desperation I pull the sword back, then throw it forward in a high, sweeping arc.

'Alfie!' I yell. 'Catch!'

The Sword of Reckoning gleams with icy green light as it spins through the air like the scythe of Death himself. It clears the clutching forest of laundry and smacks down into Alfie's outstretched hand.

'Yeah, baby!' Alfie crows in triumph. There's a blur of movement and suddenly three severed tentacles are sinking into the lint.

The kraken bellows its rage. Dozens more tentacles explode from the fluff, surging at Alfie with deadly ferocity.

But Alfie's too quick. He slashes and whirls, ducks and spins and slashes again. The Sword of Reckoning weaves a glittering pattern of destruction, leaving ribbons of laundry fluttering in its wake.

My mouth drops open. I've never seen anything like it in my life.

Leaping, whirling and spinning like a ninja, Alfie

fights his way through the tentacles and backs towards me, waving the sword at the now-wary monster.

'You all right?' he asks.

I dodge a flying tentacle, which Alfie slashes off. How cool is this guy? I can't believe I got mad at him before.

'Fine,' I say with a grin. 'Where'd you learn to fight like that, anyway?'

Alfie shrugs. 'Playing *Sword of Fury.*'

A tentacle taps me on the shoulder. I whirl and dodge, but another tentacle sneaks up from the other side and grabs the meteor scarf from my pocket.

'Hey!' I shout. 'That's mine.' I grab the scarf and heave.

The kraken heaves back.

I brace my knees and pull harder. Big mistake.

Because the kraken suddenly lets go, and before I know it, I'm flat on my back under half a metre of lint. My shocked gasp draws a clot of choking fluff deep into my throat. I try to cough but that makes it worse. My chest spasms, and in my pain and panic the slender unconscious thread of magic between me and the Globe of Tarimos is broken.

The light winks out, leaving me blind in the smothering darkness.

A tentacle snakes around my waist.

I don't even have enough breath left to scream.

CHAPTER 17

In the end, it's the kraken that saves me.

The tentacle around my waist pulls me out of the suffocating lint and lifts me high in the air. I cough up a lint ball the size of a cat and suddenly I can breathe again. I suck air like a drowning swimmer and struggle in vain to break the tentacle's grip.

Far below, the Sword of Reckoning sweeps a glowing line through the darkness. But then I hear a choking cry and the sword blinks out.

Light! We need light.

I summon a panicky burst of magic and snap my fingers, but in my hurry, I've mixed up the spells. Instead of summoning the Globe of Tarimos, I've cast the candle-lighting spell. A tiny flame flickers to life in the gap between my forefinger and thumb.

A flame. In the middle of a giant fire trap.

Am I the world's worst apprentice or what?

The tiny flame isn't as bright as the globe, but it's bright enough to see . . .

The kraken.

Its nightmare bulk is terrifyingly close. I'm hanging upside down, directly above the monster's gaping maw. I can see straight down its throat, a churning, laundry-filled chasm lined with rows and rows of stiletto-heeled shoes, all glinting and clacking like teeth. Its hot, dry breath washes over me, filling my nose with a sickening blast of lavender, as it roars out its hunger.

Okay, *now* I can scream.

I let rip with a lung-busting shriek loud enough to deafen a banshee. I'm going to die – eaten by an animated pile of dirty laundry. And not just me. Alfie's going to die, too. And Grandpa. And Bruce – well, maybe not Bruce, but—

And then I get mad. The lock of hair on my forehead coils like a whip and I take all the fear, all the frustration, all the anger, and I push it into that tiny, accidental flame between my thumb and my finger. And the tiny flame grows into a globe of fire the size of a tennis ball.

'Eat this, you overgrown octopus!' I scream.

And I hurl the ball of fire straight at the monster.

Which is all good in theory. But if you've ever hurled a fireball at a monster while hanging upside down above a chasm of stiletto teeth, you'll know it's super tough to aim. I'm wide by a mile. Worse, when my fireball lands, it sets the lint aflame.

The kraken roars and flings me high into the air.

I smack down into the fluff, then stagger to my feet as fire races towards me.

'Alfie!' I yell, peering desperately into the flames.

I can't see him.

High above me, the kraken bellows and thrashes, then plunges into the lint and disappears.

Smoke stings my eyes and I throw up a hand to shield my face from the heat. 'Alfie!'

I stumble and go down on one knee.

Suddenly Alfie's there, the Sword of Reckoning shining like a beacon in his hand. 'Wednesday!' he gasps, grabbing the back of my shirt and hauling me to my feet. 'Where's the exit?'

'It's this way,' I reply, and together we half-carry, half-drag each other out of the lint trap and along the corridor until we reach clear air.

I collapse to the floor, coughing and gasping.

Alfie shrugs off his schoolbag, sheathes the Sword of Reckoning and sinks down beside me.

'Is it gone?' he asks. 'Did you kill it?'

I shudder and drag in a shaky breath. 'I don't think it can be killed. Not unless it runs out of laundry.'

I stare blankly down the corridor. It's more of the same. More of the same endlessly intersecting melamine walls, the same chrome hooks, the same infinite selection of lost and abandoned laundry items.

More, more, more of the same rotten, stinking, endless maze.

Suddenly it's all too much.

'Oh!' I wail. 'I hate this place.' Bruce was right, wherever he is. 'We're never getting out of here.'

'Hey.' Alfie looks at me, his eyes filled with concern. 'It's okay.'

'No, it's not. It's not okay.' My lip trembles. 'I've lost the ring and Bruce is missing and now we're going to die and it's all my fault. I'm a lousy sorcerer and a terrible friend.' And now I'm full-on blubbering, with the tears and the snot and everything, and I hate it, but I can't stop. 'I'm so sorry, Alfie. I'm sorry I dragged you into this. I'm sorry about your hair. I'm sorry about everything.'

'Hey, hey.' Alfie scooches over and puts his arm around my shoulder, but that only makes me cry harder.

After a minute or two I wind down, and Alfie pulls out a snowy-white hankie. I dab my eyes and blow my nose, feeling embarrassed.

'Okay, listen,' Alfie says. 'I've got three things to say to you. Number one? You didn't drag me into anything.'

'But—'

'No, *listen*. I've travelled through a wormhole to a parallel universe, okay? I've met a Tooth Fairy. I've wielded a sword of power and battled a nightmare creature of the deep. Are you kidding me?' He grins like he's just discovered a new prime number. 'This is the best day of my life!'

Okay, fair enough. I guess if you look at it that way. But of course, he's left out the part where it might also be the last day of his life.

'Number two,' Alfie says. 'I may not know anything about magic, but I know this. You are going to be a *great* sorcerer.'

'Yeah, right.' I shake my head. 'I can't even work a stupid light spell.'

'Well, so what?' The heat in Alfie's voice surprises me. 'You need to cut yourself some slack. Your grandpa's had hundreds of years to learn that stuff. You think he could summon mystic fire when he was your age? Pff.' He waves his hand. 'In his dreams.'

And you know what? I'm actually starting to feel better. 'What was the third thing?' I ask.

'Hmm?'

'You said you had three things to say to me.'

'Oh. Did I?' Alfie looks embarrassed. 'Well, okay. The third thing is this.' He pauses, then says in a low, fierce voice, 'You are *not* a terrible friend. You're smart. You're brave. You're funny. You can do magic!' He looks at the floor. 'You're the best friend I've ever had.'

Darn it. Now I'm crying again.

'As a matter of fact,' Alfie continues, 'you're the *only* friend I've ever had.' He clears his throat. 'I've been told video game characters don't count.'

I stare at him. He's still looking at the floor. 'Alfie . . .'

He shrugs. 'Who wants to hang out with a kid whose idea of a fun time is memorising prime numbers while nitpicking the scientific inaccuracies of old *X-Files* episodes?'

'Hey,' I say quietly.

Alfie looks up.

'I do,' I say. 'That's who.'

Alfie looks at me for a moment, then his face breaks into a brilliant smile. 'Too right, you do.' He pulls himself to his feet and checks his watch. 'So, what do you say? We still have four hours and three minutes to rescue your grandpa.' He offers me his hand. 'Why don't we keep going? Like you said, we might get lucky.'

I sniff and wipe my eyes, then grab his hand and haul myself up. Because, you know what? He's right. Technically, we're not even lost. We may be trapped in the middle of a spherical insanity maze in a magically generated pocket dimension inside a parallel universe, but we know exactly how to find our way out.

All we have to do is follow the wall until we find the exit.

Of course, the trick is to do that before we die of thirst. Before Gorgomoth banishes Grandpa to his Pit of Extreme Discomfort. Before the world as we know it is taken over by a ruthless, tyrannical goblin king with unspeakable personal hygiene. Plus it's nearly ten o'clock. Our parents are going to kill us.

'Let's run,' I tell Alfie. Because time is totally running out.

We run, and in minutes we're gasping for breath, but we don't stop. My heart flutters in my chest, too fast and then too slow, but there's nothing I can do but keep running.

The Globe of Tarimos, meanwhile, bobs effortlessly above us. I get the feeling it's unimpressed with our fitness.

Wait a second . . .

If we know *how* to find the way out, but we're just not fast enough, then all we need is something that can get the job done faster. Like, oh, I don't know. A super-fast robot with a battery that never wears out?

Or a magical ball of light. I mean, what's faster than light, right?

And if I can teach the Globe of Tarimos to *Heel*, and to *Brighten*, and to *Rise*, then maybe I can teach it to do something more complicated.

Maybe I can teach it to *Navigate*.

CHAPTER 18

I stop so fast Alfie nearly ruptures a ligament trying not
to crash into me.

'What's wrong?' he asks.

'Nothing,' I say. 'I've got an idea.'

I quickly explain my idea, then close my eyes and
reach for the magic. Then I open my eyes, pump some
magic into the Globe of Tarimos and say, *'Navigate.'*

The globe hovers in mid-air, flickering like a dodgy
light bulb.

I pump in some more magic. The globe brightens
and the flickering stops.

'Navigate.'

The globe hesitates. Then it does a little left-right
hop. Did it just shrug at me?

I close my eyes again, and this time I really concentrate. I visualise the maze. Then I picture the Globe

of Tarimos navigating the maze, finding the way out. I focus on the vision until it's as sharp and clear as a splinter of glass.

Then I release the magic and say, '*Navigate!*'

The little globe zips away.

'Quick!'

Alfie and I race after it, following the globe along the corridor. It's working!

But at the very first intersection, it stops.

'*Navigate*,' I say, but it doesn't respond.

Alfie drags his fingers through his hair. 'Maybe it's confused.'

'Maybe.' I sag with fatigue, and the Globe of Tarimos sags with me, glimmering dully like a day-old glowstick. 'I told the magic what I wanted. I don't know what else to do.'

Alfie shrugs. 'Well, maybe that only works for simple stuff. You know? Maybe for something like this, it's not enough just to tell it what you want. Maybe you have to tell it how.'

I frown. 'What do you mean?'

'Well, I was thinking about Alfie Junior. He can do all kinds of amazing stuff. Like navigate a maze, or dance the Macarena.' He grins and busts out a few quick dance moves. 'But he can't do anything until I write a program to tell him how – one step at a time.'

He hitches his schoolbag. 'Too bad you can't write a program for your mind. You know, to control the magic.'

'Yeah, too bad.'

Wait, what? Rewind the tape . . .

Alfie staggers back, shielding his eyes, and for a brief panicky moment I wonder if the flash of inspiration I've just had has set my *own* hair on fire. But then I realise it's only the Globe of Tarimos. Mirroring my excitement, the little orb has lit up like a beacon and is now hovering over my head like a cartoon light bulb.

Which is absolutely fitting – because Alfie has just given me the most brilliant idea in the entire history of brilliant ideas.

I'm going to do it.

I'm going to write a program for my mind.

'Alfie, you're a genius!' Popping with excitement, I grab Alfie and lift him off his feet in a huge hug.

He squirms free with a smile. 'You know it.'

'Sure do. Now let's get out of here.' I snap my fingers and the Globe of Tarimos zips down to hover in front of me, vibrating with excitement. I sit on the floor, cross my legs and close my eyes.

This is going to be tricky.

I reach out. The magic's there, but it's different this time. Instead of a lake of lava it feels like a river flowing past me, cool and deep and powerful. I let the magic flow into me, and this time I don't try to hold it in.

I just let it flow. My skin tingles as the magic washes over me, around me and through me.

All right. I think I'm ready. It's time to tell the magic what to do, like I tried to before. But this time's going to be different. Nothing's going to blow up. No Harbour Bridges are going to burn. Because this time, I'm going to tell it *how*.

I imagine a palette of coloured blocks, like the ones in the app from robotics class. One block to move forward. Another block to stop when it reaches an intersection. A third set of blocks to decide which way to turn. And one more, to repeat the whole thing until it reaches the exit.

A magical program for navigating a maze.

Then I think for a moment and add a couple of extra blocks to finish it off.

Something rustles in the distance, but I don't dare open my eyes. This is the most complicated sorcery I've ever attempted – not to mention our last hope of getting out of here alive. Everything has to be perfect. Clearing everything else from my mind, I concentrate on the spell until every piece is locked in place, sharp and clear like they're etched in glass.

At last it's ready.

I open my eyes and the magic pours out of me in a long, rolling surge.

'*Navigate*,' I whisper.

The spell ripples through the air and plunges into the Globe of Tarimos with a high, clear note like the chime of a crystal bowl. For a moment, the globe hangs in the air, vibrating gently. Then it turns bright red and rockets away down the corridor, leaving us in complete darkness.

I hear the rustling again, closer this time.

'Um, Wednesday?' Alfie says, but I don't dare interrupt the spell.

I hold my breath. Please let it work . . .

After ten long seconds of darkness, the globe comes rocketing back. In the sudden brightness, I see two scarves and a long-sleeved robe twitch at the end of the corridor. I hear the clacking of stiletto heels and smell burnt nylon. We don't have much time.

The globe flips from red to white and hovers in front of me, bobbing with excitement.

Alfie stares at it. 'Did it find the way out?'

'I think so,' I say.

The Globe of Tarimos bounces up and down, like it's nodding.

'But we can't follow it,' Alfie says. 'It's too fast.'

'No, it's not.' I smile. 'It's not fast enough.'

Alfie looks confused, but I know what I'm doing. I hope.

I channel more magic into the globe and say, *'Faster.'*

The globe turns red and zips away again. This time it only takes three seconds to return. The rustling and clacking grow louder, closer. Halfway down the hall, a taffeta ballgown swirls in a non-existent breeze.

'Um, Wednesday?' Alfie says again. 'Did you see that?'

I did see it. But I can't afford to lose my focus.

'Faster.' I keep pouring magic into the spell, and the little globe keeps zipping away and coming back, over and over, getting faster and faster until it blurs into an unbroken ribbon of light. The vivid red ribbon ripples outwards like a wave, and, for a moment, above us and all around, the whole vast spherical maze glows red.

Thanks to my magic program, the Globe of Tarimos is now exploring the entire maze, following every possible path, over and over again, at the speed of light.

But it's not done yet.

Remember those extra code blocks I added? Just a little something to weigh up all those paths and pick the shortest one.

Suddenly the red lines disappear, leaving a single shining ribbon of blue.

The way out.

Alfie's eyes look like they're about to pop from his head.

I reach out and take his hand – just as the laundry kraken forms in front of our eyes, its new body writhing up from a random collection of laundry on the walls and floor. It whips a knotted tentacle at Alfie, but I pull him away just in time.

'Run!' I yell.

We sprint down the corridor, following the glowing ribbon of blue light.

A tremor rolls through the carpet of odd socks as the laundry kraken roars its frustration behind us.

'How did you *do* that?' Alfie asks as we run. 'No, wait. Don't tell me.'

We slam around a corner. Seconds later, there's a thunderous crash behind us. I whip a glance over my shoulder. The kraken is using its tentacles to pull itself along the corridor, *schlorping* after us with terrifying speed.

I put my head down and pour on more speed.

'Random . . . mouse . . . algorithm?' Alfie puffs. 'No, that can't be . . . right. Pledge? But that wouldn't . . . account for . . .'

A flailing tentacle flies at my ankles. I hurdle it and keep sprinting.

'Of course!' Alfie shouts. 'Trémaux's algorithm!'

We stagger forward, fighting our way through the drift of odd socks piling in front of us, pushed forward by the surging monster like the bow wave of a ship.

'Am I right?' Alfie pants. 'I'm right, aren't I? Wednesday?'

'Just run!' I scream.

We sprint around a corner into a long, empty corridor. White light spills through a tall doorway at the end.

'The exit!' I yell.

We charge forward, the kraken flailing at our heels. Clutching tentacles surge around us.

The doorway's right ahead. We're going to make it.

Then a tentacle locks around my ankle and I'm falling, and Alfie's falling with me. More tentacles close around us, dragging us down. But our momentum carries us forward.

Side by side, we tumble through the doorway. As we cross the threshold, the Globe of Tarimos winks out, and the kraken's grip instantly releases. We spill onto a brightly lit expanse of pristine, white-tiled floor.

We're out of the maze.

I scramble frantically away from the exit, but the only sign of the laundry kraken is a tangled pile of clothing lying in the doorway.

Alfie brushes himself off and cautiously approaches the pile.

'Careful,' I say.

'It's all right,' Alfie says. 'It's gone. And look!'

He stoops and picks something up out of the pile. It's a navy-blue bucket hat.

'Succulent!' Alfie plonks the hat on his head and wanders over to me.

I look around. We're standing in some sort of cavernous circular cathedral. Open doorways dot the perimeter of the room for as far as we can see. Large signs mark the top of each doorway: **LOOSE CHANGE. CAR KEYS. USED DENTAL FLOSS.** I even spot a doorway labelled **POWER-MAD ADVERSARIES.** I turn to look at the doorway we came through. Its sign reads: **LOST IN THE WASH.**

Hmm. That sounds about right.

Another, smaller sign posted next to the doorway reads: **REMEMBER! YOU** *are the* **FAERY** *responsible for* **YOUR SAFETY!** Underneath which, someone has added, *Please do not release the kraken.*

The huge room is teeming with summer faeries with their wildly coloured hair and glorious wings, and winter faeries too, all tall and proud and silver-haired. Everyone's dressed in the same white uniform. They rush around, carrying laundry baskets and coat hangers, pushing trolleys, sorting clothes pegs.

High above us, a huge stainless-steel tub spins and sparkles like a black hole. Every few seconds something is ejected from this strange chandelier at high speed, whizzing through the air and out through one of the doors.

Suddenly, a faery with long silver hair points in our direction and yells, 'Intruders!'

Every faery in the room stops and stares at us.

Oh, boy.

Here we go again.

CHAPTER 19

The thunder of stampeding feet grows behind us as we sprint around the enormous circular sorting chamber, pursued by an angry mob of faeries.

Signposted doorways flash past as we run. **PET HAIR. BUS PASSES. MOVIE STUBS. ALL-POWERFUL MAGICAL ITEMS.**

Wait. That sounds like us.

'This way!' I'm sprinting hard when we pelt through the doorway, which is why I run straight into the counter.

Ouch. This department is smaller than I expected. By the time I gather my senses and get to my feet, Alfie's standing at the counter, which is empty except for an enormous green plant in a small golden pot.

Behind the counter, a young summer faery with golden skin, shimmering golden wings, nose piercings and a pink-and-green striped mohawk is sitting on a stool, chewing a toothpick. On the wall behind her are hundreds of hooks, all of them empty.

All except one.

There, gleaming red, the only all-powerful magical item to end up lost in the **ALL-POWERFUL MAGICAL ITEMS** department of the Realm of Lost Things, is the Ruby Ring.

'Where'd they go?' a voice yells from somewhere outside.

I pull Grandpa's ticket from my pocket and shove it in front of the mohawked faery. 'Um, excuse me? I think my grandpa has an account here?'

The faery waves a hand at the ticket and it sparkles with green. 'He sure does,' she says, with the toothpick still in her teeth. She indicates the board behind her. 'Which item do you want to collect?'

I dance from foot to foot in frustration. Clearly there's only one item to collect, so why even ask? Can't she see we're in a—

Alfie touches my arm.

I take a deep breath. 'Just the ring, please. And may I say, I love your hair.'

'Really?' The faery tucks the toothpick behind her ear. At the same time, the pot plant on the counter seems to flutter. 'Hey, thanks. You're literally the first person to say anything nice to me all day.' She shakes her head. 'Faeries these days, you know? It's just hair, people! Why shouldn't I experiment a little?' Her voice cracks and the pot plant sags.

I feel a surge of sympathy. 'I totally get you,' I say. 'I was born with this.' I touch the ice-blue lock of hair at my forehead.

She nods. 'Love it.'

'Thanks. But you wouldn't believe the hassle I get about it at school. Like, really? Like you said, it's just hair.'

'Exactly!' She gives me a big smile, and I swear, the pot plant seems to grow an inch. 'I'm Adaline, by the way. Great to meet you.' She glances at my forehead, and I know what she's seeing. Nothing. My eyebrows are no more. I wait for her to say something, but she doesn't.

'I'm Wednesday,' I say.

Alfie gives her a big smile. 'And I'm Alfie.'

Adaline leans over to collect the ring from the hook, but then pauses. 'You sure you don't want the cloak as well?'

'Pardon?'

'Your grandfather's cloak,' Adaline says, pointing at an empty hook on the now-empty board.

'This way!' an angry voice cries, way too close for comfort. 'Don't let them get away!'

'Ah, Wednesday?' Alfie says. 'Any minute now would be great.'

It takes all my strength to stop the hopping back-and-forth thing again. 'Sure,' I say to Adaline. 'Thanks. Great. The cloak too, please. Only, could you make it quick?'

Adaline smiles and reaches for the board again. The air below her hand seems to ripple, as if disturbed by the movement of a long piece of invisible fabric.

'There you go, babe,' she says, handing me the ring.

I slide it onto my finger, but before I can try to open a portal, Adaline thrusts something else at me. The invisible thing. I can feel it, like a pair of stretchy cotton pyjamas, but I can't see it.

Adaline gives me a wink. 'He's always losing it. I like to keep it around as long as I can. You never know when an invisibility cloak will come in handy, know what I mean?'

I lean over to give Adaline a huge hug. 'You're a lifesaver. And I really do love the hair.'

The faery's pointed ears flush green. The pot plant shivers with pleasure. 'Thanks.' She looks over my shoulder, then gives me a wink and whispers, 'You might want to put that on and nip behind the counter right about now.'

I give the invisibility cloak a swirl, and Alfie and I crouch beneath it. It's large enough to cover us both, and lighter than it feels, like gossamer, but it smells distinctly like the ocean. Could be a new laundry powder scent, or maybe Grandpa last wore it snorkelling in Drowned Atlantis.

We start to creep behind Adaline's **ALL-POWERFUL MAGICAL ITEMS** counter, but we only make it halfway when a bunch of winter faeries in full armour come busting in. I recognise the faery leading the charge. It's the tall, cold faery captain, the one Bruce called Shnooky-pumpkin.

And speaking of Bruce, I'm starting to miss the old bone. I sure hope he's all right.

Captain Shnooky strides up to the counter and raps on the counter. 'You there!' she barks at Adaline. 'Which way did they go?'

Adaline leans back on her stool and narrows her eyes. 'Excuse me?'

The pot plant shivers its leaves, making an angry rattling noise.

Captain Shnooky stares at the pot plant for a second, then clears her throat. 'We're hunting two human intruders.' Her icy, blue-eyed gaze sweeps the room and stops when it reaches Alfie and me, crouching motionless under the invisibility cloak.

I feel sick. It could be the ocean smell. I hate boats. Right now I'd give my not-yet-regrown eyebrows if I could just portal to my couch. I try swiping with the Ruby Ring a few times, concentrating hard. Nothing.

Alfie tenses beside me and I realise Shnooky is still staring right at us. She can't see us, can she? But then I remember the way the air rippled when Adaline picked up the cloak and suddenly it seems like a really good idea to stay very, very still. It seems to work, because

Captain Shnooky finally turns away and steps up to check behind Adaline's counter.

'Humans, eh?' Adaline arches an eyebrow. 'They sound super-dangerous.' She flicks a glance at the other soldiers standing awkwardly in the doorway. 'No wonder there are so many of you.'

The captain scowls. 'Where did they go?'

Adaline shrugs. 'How should I know? I'm supposed to stay behind the counter, learn some responsibility, remember?' She pulls the toothpick out from behind her ear and flicks it through her fingers like a spinning top.

Captain Shnooky makes a disgusted sound, like if the back of your throat could roll its eyes. She turns to the other faeries. 'Come on, we're wasting our time.'

Alfie and I stand frozen, hardly daring to breathe. Adaline blows kisses as the faeries retreat. 'Always a pleasure, Captain. Do come again.'

We wait another minute, Adaline flicking the toothpick around her fingers. Then she laughs. 'The old invisibility cloak trick! Gets them every time.'

I lift the edge of the cloak over my head, so the mohawked faery can feel the full strength of my gratitude. 'That was AMAZING.'

'Totally molten,' Alfie agrees.

Adaline waves away our thanks. 'Ah, it's the least I could do. Those soldier faeries, always throwing their armour around. Sometimes I like to mess with them, you know?' She grins. 'Anyways, you two had better make your escape.'

But we can't escape yet. Because we're not two. We're two and a bit – an annoying, snarky, eyelight-rolling bit.

'How long?' I ask Alfie.

He checks his watch. 'Three hours, eighteen minutes.'

It's tight, but I hope it'll be enough.

'Actually,' I say to Adaline. 'I was wondering . . . You've been so helpful already, but . . .'

Adaline's face lights up. 'You need new outfits, right? I didn't want to say anything, but pantaloons are *so* last century. If you want new threads, you've come to the right gal.' She winks. 'There are certain perks that come with working in a laundry.'

I can't help smiling at her enthusiasm. 'Thanks, but what we really need is to find our friend.'

Adaline leans in. 'There's another human loose in the laundry?'

'Sort of,' Alfie says. 'More like a cranium.'

We explain the situation with Bruce, and Adaline zaps away to make a few enquiries. She's back in minutes with good news, and with new clothes as well.

'I think I know where to find your skull,' she says, guarding the door while we take turns getting changed. It's tricky to dress under an invisibility cloak, but given the absence of change rooms, it's also super-convenient.

Suddenly I understand why Grandpa might take this cloak to the beach.

When we're done, Adaline admires our new threads. 'You guys!' she exclaims.

She has Alfie in black lace-up boots, steel-grey jeans, a black T-shirt and a white bomber jacket. 'Are you sure?' he asks, clearly uncomfortable in a collarless shirt.

'Totally! And wear both belts,' Adaline instructs, handing him one in blue, the other in brown. 'It looks killer, plus you never know when an extra belt might come in handy.'

He agrees, but only if he gets to keep his navy-blue bucket hat with its Atomic Energy merit badge. This, along with his schoolbag and the Sword of Reckoning, does kind of . . . personalise the whole look.

Wednesday by Adaline is simple but classic. I'm in high-top sneakers, skinny black jeans, a white tee and a denim jacket. There's no space in the pockets of my jeans for anything bigger than a paperclip, so I pop the winkleberry carefully into my jacket. Then Adaline offers us each a pair of aviator sunnies.

'But we're inside,' I point out.

'That should never stop anyone from wearing sunglasses,' she says. 'Now, let's go find your skull.'

CHAPTER 20

If you'd asked me to list the major hazards of being invisible – before I got to actually try it, that is – I probably would have come up with things like tripping over my own feet, scaring the neighbour's cat, or accidentally getting run over while trying to cross the road. Constantly getting my toes stepped on wouldn't even have made the top five.

Then again, how was I to know that my first taste of the wonders of invisibility would involve being squashed cheek-to-cheek with Alfie under a too-small cloak, like a couple of untrained and terminally clumsy tango dancers?

I choke down a yelp as Alfie's big black boot comes down hard on my instep for the thirtieth time.

'Sorry,' he whispers.

I mutter something about size-fifty feet and we continue our awkward, shuffling progress across the enormous circular sorting chamber at the heart of the Laundry Fairy Dry Cleaners.

We're following Adaline as the golden-winged faery strolls casually through the controlled chaos of the sorting chamber. The magic of the invisibility cloak makes everything outside look grey and shadowy. Or it could be my sunglasses.

'It looks like your friend has been sorted into an old department,' Adaline murmurs. 'One of the oldest. And this place has been around since the First Age.' She sidesteps to avoid being flattened by a huge trolley full of polka-dotted underpants being shoved along by a frazzled-looking faery with silver wings and hair the colour of autumn leaves, then resumes her stroll across the concourse.

Alfie and I shuffle after her, wide-eyed. Everywhere there are faeries in motion, scrubbing the floor, hanging underpants, darning socks and jumpers, sewing extra pockets and clever hems.

Adaline stops in front of a tall, arched doorway built from roughly mortared hand-cut stones. 'This is it,' she murmurs.

I read the sign carved into the ancient, time-worn keystone at the top of the arch.

'Is this a joke?' I whisper.

Adaline shrugs. 'The whole system's automatic, so I can't be sure. But tell me that doesn't sound like your guy.'

I peer at the sign again. Even diffused by the shimmering grey haze of the invisibility cloak and faded by the passage of millennia, the lettering is unmistakable. I read it again, just to make sure.

SNARKY UNDEAD ENTITIES

'That's Bruce, all right,' Alfie says.

Adaline leans against the wall beside the archway and retrieves her toothpick from behind her ear. 'As far as I know,' she murmurs, 'this department's never been occupied. But I've heard stories. It could be dangerous.'

Alfie gulps. 'Dangerous?'

'I wish I could come with you,' Adaline says, 'but . . .'

Her golden eyes flick to a nearby faery in an all-white suit with a badge that says **SUPERVISOR** in huge, over-sized letters. The faery is watching her, arms folded like a tall, grumpy statue.

'That's okay,' I tell her. 'We'll take it from here.'

Adaline gives a barely perceptible nod and pops the toothpick into her mouth. 'Be careful, okay?'

'Thanks, Adaline,' I say. 'We totally owe you.'

'Don't be silly.' Adaline grins. 'Laters!'

Her golden wings blur into motion and she flies away, spiralling through the air like a pink-and-green-haired hummingbird. Her laughter carries back to us as she swoops low over the supervisor faery, forcing her to duck for cover in a most undignified manner.

We shuffle through the doorway. As we move down the corridor, the white-tiled floor of the concourse gives way to rough-hewn granite flagstones. The walls change from efficient-white to a mosaic of grey and cream stones. As soon as we're out of sight, we stash the invisibility cloak and our sunnies in Alfie's backpack. I keep the ring on my finger. Just knowing we have it back gives me a curious kind of confidence.

The corridor winds deeper into the darkness. Torches in iron brackets flame magically to life as we approach, then extinguish themselves as we pass.

'Strange kind of laundry,' Alfie says.

I nod. 'She did say it was old.'

The passageway ends at a blank wall, also constructed of carefully stacked stones. An arch in the wall looks like it might be a doorway, but it's blocked by more stone, this time a solid slab.

A small sign next to the archway reads:

WARNING

The contents of this fullonica are protected
by a time lock.

Failure to open the fullonica within the allocated time
may result in CERTAIN DOOM.

We apologise for any inconvenience.

I frown. 'Fullonica?'

Alfie's eyes go wide. 'Certain doom?'

Where have I heard the word 'fullonica' before? It tickles at the back of my mind, but I can't think of an answer. Maybe because all I can think about now is 'CERTAIN DOOM'. So much for confidence.

A waist-high iron lever stands beside the door, sticking out of a slot in the floor.

'What do you reckon?' I ask Alfie.

Alfie looks at me. 'If Bruce is in there? Go for it.'

I grab the lever and pull. It resists for a moment, as though stiff from centuries of disuse, then falls forward with a clank. From behind the wall there's a muffled ratcheting of chains and then, with a sound like the grinding of a great millstone, the stone slab rises slowly up.

Cool air washes out through the archway like a lonely ghost. Beyond the doorway is silence and echoing darkness.

I peer into the shadows, senses alert. The back of my neck prickles and the blue-white lock of hair stirs on my forehead. Okay, this feels like a trap. I mean, seriously. It couldn't feel more like a trap if the entrance was marked with a big block of cheese.

I think back to Adaline . . . how much can we really trust her? But then I remember the way she hid us from

Captain Shnooky. If she wanted to trap us, she could've done it already.

And we can't leave without Bruce.

I look at Alfie. Alfie looks at me. Then he slips off his schoolbag and draws the Sword of Reckoning. I conjure the Globe of Tarimos and hold it in my left hand, its pale glow a comforting presence. Then I reach for the magic and draw it in, ready to slam mystic fire at anything that dares threaten us. Or, at least try to.

Side by side, we step through the archway.

Torches leap into flame all around, revealing a high-vaulted, eight-sided chamber built of stacked stone bricks. The floor is a great octagon, about forty metres across and paved in grey tiles. The ceiling is flat grey stone, at least fifteen metres above our heads. To the right, a tall, funnel-shaped glass tank, like the top half of an hourglass, rests in an ornate golden stand about three metres above the ground. The tank is filled with some kind of clear yellow liquid. To the left are eight table-high stone plinths like a row of barstools. The top of each plinth is hollowed into a bowl.

Apart from that, the chamber is empty.

'No Bruce,' Alfie says, taking it all in.

But on the far wall of the chamber is a second door. It's enormous and eight-sided, maybe made of some sort of iron. It stands closed, like the entrance to a colossal bank vault.

'Behind there,' I guess. 'That looks like—'

BOOM!

The floor shakes as the stone door behind us falls shut with a deafening crash.

CHAPTER 21

I spin, my heart pounding like a sackful of jazz drummers, expecting trapdoors or floor spikes or swarms of giant cockroaches.

Don't ask me why cockroaches. The place just has that kind of vibe, I guess.

Anyway, there's nothing like that. Just the quiet sound of metal sliding against metal as, one by one, eight huge iron bolts slip into place around the octagonal iron door.

As the last bolt locks into position, a valve clicks open in the hourglass-shaped tank and yellow liquid starts pouring out in a thin, steady stream. The stream of liquid spatters on the floor and runs down a drain hole.

'Ah, nuts,' I growl. 'It *is* a trap.'

Alfie stares at the vault door, then at the liquid streaming from the tank. 'Not a trap. A time lock.'

'We're already running out of time,' I complain. 'How are we supposed to—'

'Over here.' Alfie sheathes his sword and hurries across to the tank.

Two golden pitchers hang from hooks on the ornately carved tank stand. Each pitcher has a slender, rounded shape with a narrow neck, a flat base and a pair of curved handles. The larger of the two has the number 5 marked on its side in delicate silver inlay. The smaller pitcher is marked with the number 3.

Alfie unhooks the 5 pitcher and holds it thoughtfully. 'Five and three,' he says. He walks over to the row of plinths with their carved stone bowls and traces a finger down the side of the nearest plinth. For the first time, I notice the plinths are all numbered, 1 to 8, the numerals cut deeply into the white stone.

'Eight bolts,' Alfie says. 'Eight bowls. Five and three.' He snaps his fingers. 'It's a jug problem.'

I frown. 'A what?'

Alfie throws a worried glance at the glass tank. The yellow liquid is emptying fast. He holds his jug under the stream. As it fills, he says, 'Eight bowls, right? One for each bolt on the door. I'm guessing we're meant to use these jugs to unlock Bruce. We just need to measure the right amount of liquid into each bowl.'

Oh, is that all? I stare at the giant door with its eight huge bolts, then at the eight plinths with their eight identical bowls. 'But what's the right amount of liquid?'

Alfie's jug is full. He steps back, holding it carefully. 'That's the problem. Now fill yours.'

I unhook the 3 pitcher and hold it under the stream. The floor beneath the tank is already splattered with slippery yellow liquid.

'Make sure you fill it all the way,' Alfie says. 'I'm guessing every drop counts.'

When my jug is full, I carry it to the row of plinths. I reach Alfie just as he finishes emptying his 5 jug into the bowl carved into the 5 plinth.

Nothing happens.

'Now what?' I ask.

Alfie looks around. His eyes fall on an iron lever standing next to the plinth. 'Here we go,' he says happily, and pulls the lever.

For a second, nothing happens. But if Alfie's right, we've just added the perfect volume of liquid to the bowl. So *something* should happen, right?

And then it does.

With a deep, grinding sound, the entire plinth sinks into the floor. At the same time, one of the bolts on the huge octagonal door retracts into its socket.

We've unlocked the first bolt.

'Brilliant!' I carry my 3 jug to the 3 plinth and empty it into the bowl.

Alfie trots back to the tank and starts refilling his pitcher.

As soon as the last drops of yellow liquid pour out of my pitcher, I yank the lever.

The 3 plinth sinks into the floor and another bolt retracts.

Two down! Confidence surges through me. Maybe we'll avoid certain doom after all.

'Let's do the 8 next,' Alfie says.

We refill both pitchers, empty them into the 8 bowl and pull the lever. The plinth sinks into the floor and another bolt retracts.

Three down, five to go. I step back and look at the row of plinths. We still have 1, 2, 4, 6 and 7 to do.

'Now what?' I ask. Our jugs only hold three and five units. 'Maybe I could fill my jug one-third of the way, then we could—'

'Sorry, Wednesday,' Alfie interrupts. 'I'm pretty sure it works by weight. Some kind of balance mechanism hidden under the floor, probably. Which means we need to be accurate. If it's even a few grams too heavy or too light . . .' Alfie makes a face. 'We'll be on our way to a hot date with certain doom.'

I frown, imagining a big old-fashioned pair of scales. 'A balance, huh? What makes you think that?'

Alfie grins. 'That's how I'd do it.'

Fair enough. Between the inside-out spherical wardrobe maze and this needlessly complex numerically themed time lock, I'm starting to detect a distinct whiff of crazed mathematical genius in the fiendish mind responsible for designing this place.

Luckily, I have a mathematical genius of my own.

'Subtraction!' Alfie exclaims, snapping his fingers with excitement.

I blink. 'Pardon?'

Alfie grabs the 5 jug and holds it under the yellow stream. 'We used addition to fill the 8 bowl, right?' Alfie says. 'Five plus three is eight. So, five subtract three is . . . ?'

'Two!' I realise. 'Genius! But how do we—'

Alfie steps back from the tank, holding his full jug. 'So I've got five.' He starts pouring from his jug into mine, filling it all the way. 'Subtract three . . .'

'Careful,' I say as the stream of yellow liquid wavers near the lip of my jug. If Alfie's right about the mechanism, we've got to be precise. Even a minor spill would mean starting over, wasting precious minutes.

Alfie stops pouring with a flourish. He holds up his now partially empty jug in triumph. 'Leaving two!'

He pours the remaining liquid from his pitcher into the 2 bowl and pulls the lever. Another bolt retracts and the 2 plinth sinks into the grey-tiled floor.

We still have four bowls left to fill: 1, 4, 6 and 7.

We fill 4, 6 and 7 using combinations of 2 and 5.

Now there's only one bowl left. But the hourglass is emptying fast.

'How are we going to do the 1 bowl?' I ask.

Alfie scratches his head, his face pinching into a frown. 'One equals three subtract two.'

'Sure. But we don't have a two-unit jug.'

'No, but . . .'

The yellow liquid pours steadily out of the hourglass, splashing and splattering on the tiles below. It looks like we only have a few minutes left.

Alfie grins. 'I've got it! Fill the 3 jug. Quick!'

I hold the 3 jug under the rapidly emptying tank and fill it up.

Alfie picks up the 5. 'Now tip it all into here. Careful!'

I do as he says.

'Now fill it again,' Alfie says, glancing nervously at the hourglass. 'Hurry!'

I fill the 3 jug again. 'Now what?' We've got three units of liquid in each jug. 'How are we supposed to get one out of this?'

'It's three subtract two, remember?'

'But we don't *have* two.' Panic gnaws at my guts. I don't know what's going to happen if we don't get the door open before the tank runs dry, and I am *not* keen to find out – not if certain doom is involved. Plus, we could lose Bruce forever! 'We've got three in this one, and three in that one.'

'Exactly,' Alfie says with an infuriatingly calm smile. 'Three units in my five-unit jug, leaving how much empty space?'

The answer hits me like a sunrise. 'Two!'

I top up Alfie's jug with two units from my three-unit jug, leaving one unit behind.

That's it.

We've done it.

We've measured out one unit.

Clutching the pitcher, I race for the last plinth. That skull had better be grateful!

But my high-tops are slippery from the messy liquid splashing under the tank. I'm only halfway to the plinth when my foot slips sideways and I go down hard, my hip and elbow slamming against the tiles.

I let out a yelp of pain and surprise. By the time I think of the pitcher, it's already clanging across the floor, spilling its contents in a slippery yellow puddle.

'No!' Ignoring the pain flaring through my elbow, I scramble forward and snatch up the jug. We've got to refill it before the tank runs dry.

I whip around and look frantically towards the tank. It's still flowing, but the line of yellow liquid is racing towards the bottom of the funnel. How much is left? Ten units? Five? Less?

We're not going to make it.

Alfie rears up beside the tank, waving his arms and yelling, 'Throw it! Throw it!'

I swing my arm back, then whip it forward, hurling the pitcher across the room in a desperate round-arm throw. The golden jug spins through the air like a satellite, then smacks down into Alfie's waiting hands.

He shoves it under the almost-empty tank. Yellow liquid gurgles into the jug, rising with agonising slowness. The yellow stream slows to a trickle.

'Got it!' Alfie crows as the liquid reaches the top of the jug.

The stream of yellow liquid slows, dwindles, and stops.

The last few drops fall from the tank.

Drip.

Drip.

Drip.

As the final drop falls, there's a horrible, rumbling CLUNK.

'What was that?' I whisper.

Alfie shakes his head, his eyes wide with fear.

Another clunk, followed by an ominous grinding.

The ceiling starts to descend.

CHAPTER 22

My knees turn to jelly and my guts to water as the enormous stone ceiling rumbles slowly down towards us. I try to breathe deep, stay calm. We've got enough problems without adding accidental fireballs to the mix.

'Intruder alert,' a metallic voice echoes through the rapidly shrinking chamber. 'Intruder alert. Intruder alert.'

Well, that's just great. The huge octagonal slab above us is a perfect fit for the floor below. When that thing touches down there won't be enough room for a cockroach, let alone an intruder.

'Certain doom,' Alfie whispers in a hollow voice, barely audible above the sound of grinding stone and the muffled rattle of chains.

Okay, I'm *so* not ready for certain doom. But I'm wearing Grandpa's ring. I can do this.

I reach for the magic and swipe the Ruby Ring through the air. *'Open.'*

I look around for a portal. Or a mini-portal. Or something.

But there's nothing. I must be doing it wrong.

'Portal!' I command, swiping again with the ring. *'Wormhole! Voidy-thingy!'*

Nothing.

I bite down on my panic and look around the chamber, searching desperately for our next move. We have one bolt left to unlock and one bowl left to fill. The stone door through which we entered stands closed, solid and immovable. The octagonal door is also sealed tight, secured by the final bolt.

I think back to the time in Grandpa's basement, when his locked chest magically unlatched. So there's at least one opening spell I can do right.

I reach for the magic again, and this time I unleash it at the bolted iron door. *'Open!'*

Nothing so much as budges. Unless you count the ceiling, which is dropping ever closer.

I feel the panic rising again and look around for another way out. The room is bare but for the empty tank and the final plinth, which stands alone, its empty bowl calling to us like a beacon. Plinth number *1*.

It's our only chance.

I take the 3 pitcher from Alfie's trembling hand and set it down next to the 5. Both pitchers are full. That means we still have eight units of liquid – enough to fill the final bowl eight times over.

The question is, with two full jugs and no more liquid in reserve, can we accurately measure a single unit?

One thing's for sure – I'm going to need Alfie's help.

'Alfie,' I say, grabbing him by the shoulders. 'Look at me.'

His panic-filled eyes lock onto mine. I've seen that look before, when he realised there was no way the Standard Model of Particle Physics could explain baryon asymmetry.

Well, there's only one way out of a conundrum like that. Experiment.

'We can do this,' I tell him, trying to sound confident. 'We just need to get one unit into the last bowl. We've got eight units. That's enough, right?'

'Eight units?' Alfie blinks, and his eyes come back into focus. 'It should be enough, but . . .' He closes his eyes, counting rapidly on his fingers. 'No, it's impossible. It only works with a third jug. We need a third jug!'

Alfie starts to hyperventilate, his breath dragging in and out in quick, shallow gasps. 'Certain doom!' he wails. 'We're going to be squished like strawberries. And I never got to see the Bodleian Euclid!'

Uh-oh. It takes a lot to panic Alfie. And when he starts talking about the Bodleian Euclid, you know things are serious.

My left hand clenches into a fist so tight I can feel the fingernails digging into my palm.

'It's okay,' I tell him, my mind suddenly icy calm. 'I'll get you your third jug.'

I sit on the floor and close my eyes. I need to clear my mind. Which, it turns out, is easier said than done. Especially when certain doom – in the form of a five-thousand-ton granite slab – is slowly descending upon you to the metallic accompaniment of ratcheting chains.

Chains, chains.

Why chains? And why is the slab descending slowly? It must be connected to a counterweight. Somewhere, another great slab must be slowly rising into the air, the two forces almost perfectly balanced.

Forces. Balanced.

But that's it!

When Grandpa was trying to teach me to levitate a pencil, he told me to imagine an invisible string between my hand and the pencil, lifting it into the air. But here's the thing. I wasn't *really* lifting the pencil with my hand. I was lifting it with my mind. Which means that whatever upward force I applied to the pencil, the pencil was applying an equal and opposite downward force – *to my mind*.

Yikes.

No wonder it gave me a headache. I'm lucky it didn't squeeze my brain out through my nose like toothpaste. Grandpa kept telling me to watch my backswing – and now, finally, I know what he meant.

I reach for the magic, letting it pour into me like water into a jug. The unruly lock of hair stirs restlessly on my forehead. I open my eyes and extend my hands, right palm facing up and left palm facing down. This has to work, it just has to. I won't let Alfie get squished like a strawberry.

'Pour it out,' I tell him. '*Slowly.*'

Alfie nods. With trembling hands, he lifts the *3* jug and, ever-so-gently, starts to pour.

As the first drop of liquid falls from the jug, I cup my right hand, reach out with the magic and whisper, '*Levitate.*'

An invisible tendril of magical force flows out of my right hand. It curls around the yellow drop, stopping its fall, cradling it in mid-air like an invisible glass bowl.

Alfie stares at the levitating droplet. 'The third jug!' he whispers. Then he grins and keeps pouring.

I focus on the liquid, imagining it cupped in my right palm, holding it suspended in mid-air in a wobbling, shimmering hemisphere. As the hemisphere grows, I feel a painful pressure growing inside my head.

Okay, now for the tricky part.

I draw in more magic and send it through my left hand, pushing against the ground with a gentle downward force. Immediately the pressure eases and the hemisphere of liquid stabilises. Action and reaction. Forces in balance.

Triumph surges through me and the lock of hair on my forehead blazes with blue-white light, filling the chamber with a fierce radiance.

My arms tremble and my head throbs with the effort of holding the spell together, but I don't dare let up.

The ceiling grinds steadily lower.

Alfie, his eyes shining with excitement and the reflected glory of my unexpectedly luminescent hair, keeps pouring until the 3 pitcher is empty. A half-globe of liquid wobbles in the air between us like yellow jelly in an invisible bowl.

The ceiling keeps dropping. It's less than a metre above Alfie's head.

Working with steady focus, Alfie pours three units of liquid from the 5 pitcher into the 3, then dumps the rest out onto the floor. Then he positions the empty 5 pitcher next to the wobbling yellow hemisphere.

'Ready,' he says.

Ignoring the pain in my arms and the pressure in my head, I clench my teeth and pour more magic into the spell. Then I squeeze the fingers of my cupped right hand, pinching the invisible bowl of force into a shallow spout on one side.

The yellow liquid sloshes but doesn't spill. Alfie holds the 5 pitcher under the spout.

Slowly, carefully, the tendons in my arm straining like red-hot wire, I tilt my right hand. The bowl of force tilts as well, pouring the liquid in a steady stream into Alfie's jug.

'That's it!' Alfie exclaims as the last drop falls into the pitcher. 'You did it.'

I let go of the spell and the magic puffs out of me like wind-blown smoke. Black spots swim in front of my eyes as Alfie places the 5 pitcher on the ground and tops it up from pitcher 3, leaving behind a single unit of yellow liquid. The room spins, and the floor rises to meet me as Alfie races for the final plinth.

When I open my eyes, the ceiling's back where it's meant to be. Even better, both the massive stone door and the octagonal iron door are standing open. Beyond the octagonal door is a dark vault.

'That was *amazing*,' Alfie says, helping me to my feet.

I grin. 'Not as amazing as you figuring out that jug problem.'

Suddenly, in the darkness of the vault, twin pinpoints of flame kindle to light.

'What took you so long?' a familiar voice asks. 'The room service around here sucks.'

Bruce!

I'd love to say it's a joyous reunion, that we hug and butterflies rise into the sky and harps play in the background. But none of that happens. Instead, Bruce says some snarky things about my lack of eyebrows, and I respond with some other things about his lack of face.

'At least it's clean,' he retaliates. I decide not to mention the bright orange **VISITOR** sticker still slapped on top of his shiny dome. 'Never thought I'd end up in a fullonica,' he says. 'Ugh.'

I tuck Bruce under my arm and we hustle out of the vault and head for the doorway. But before we're even halfway there, the sound of marching echoes down the corridor and a squad of soldiers bursts into the room.

'Going somewhere?' their leader asks. My heart drops like a plinth through the floor. It's the faery captain.

'Shnooky-pumpkin,' Bruce says in a cold voice. 'We meet again.'

'Silence!' Captain Shnooky roars. 'You're all under arrest. Again.' She turns to me. 'So hand over the skull.'

My head is aching and the muscles in my arms feel like I've gone twenty rounds with a cave tiger. But there's no way I'm giving up Bruce, not after everything we've done to find him.

And hey, I just nailed levitation, right? So, I'm guessing this is my moment. If there was ever a time to show what I can do, it's now.

I summon the magic and wave the Ruby Ring. *'Wormhole!'* I command. *'Void! Portal! Gateway!'*

Nothing happens.

Oh, come on. Surely I can summon one pathetic interdimensional portal.

I try again. *'Exit! Doorway! Escape hatch!'*

Still nothing.

I am officially the world's worst apprentice. Now my heart aches too, and my elbow is still stinging from when I slipped and fell and nearly ruined everything. And that gives me an idea.

'Alfie!' I shout. 'With me!'

There's no time to think it through. We sprint right at Captain Shnooky and her soldiers. She's standing just inside the doorway, separated from us by a stretch of wet tiles. I've seen this sort of thing in movies, so I have no hesitation in launching myself onto the floor. I know I'll slip. I'll slip fast, too, and straight.

I'll slip right under Shnooky's legs and out into the corridor to safety, where I'll roll to my feet and keep on running. It will be glorious. It will be epic. It will be spoken of for generations.

Except I guess I misjudge the angle, because instead of slipping under the faery captain's legs, I slam into the wall next to her. Alfie spins out of control and crashes into me like a wrecking ball.

There's pain. There's lack of oxygen, driven from my lungs by the impact. And then there's just plain loss.

'Bruce!' I cry as Shnooky snatches him from my hands.

Alfie gets to his feet and helps me up. 'It was a good plan, Wednesday,' he says. 'We did our best.'

I nod and suck air into my crushed lungs. And then I wonder . . . why haven't we been clapped in chains already?

'Ready to go, Apprentice?' Shnooky asks.

What? When I look up, it's Shnooky, but not like I've ever seen before. She's holding Bruce in one hand, and her eyes are glowing. They're glowing with the same distinctive orange gleam as the eyelights that usually shine from Bruce's sockets.

Captain Shnooky turns to her soldiers. 'Dismissed,' she says, snapping her fingers. The tall, icy-white soldiers turn on their heels and march away. Then Shnooky winks at me, and hums the first line of *I Once a Wandering Wizard Knew*.

'Bruce!' Alfie exclaims. It must be. No one else could be that annoying.

'The very one,' Shnooky says, and bows, still holding the skull. 'Well done, Apprentice.'

'And Alfie,' I say. 'He did good too.' I sneak a smile at Alfie. His white jacket is now stained yellow, like my white shirt, and we're both sticky and bruised. But we're alive.

Bruce-the-skull clacks his teeth and Bruce-the-faery-captain speaks: 'Well done to both of you. But the next step won't be so easy. We're off to the Tower of Shadows.'

Alfie cheers. 'And we still have two hours and four minutes left!'

Yikes.

Captain Shnooky turns to me. 'I don't suppose I could borrow that ring?'

I hand it over. Bruce-the-faery-captain slips the Ruby Ring onto her finger. With a flash of her hand, she conjures an inky black void, then gives me back the ring.

'Step lively, Apprentice,' she says, her eyes still aglow. Then she hands me the skull and the orange light fades from her eyes.

She blinks and gives me a startled look. 'Hey, wait!'

'No, thanks,' I say with a smile. Then I hold Bruce close and grab Alfie's hand, and together we jump into the void.

CHAPTER 23

When I step out of the void, the first thing that hits me is the smell. It's thick and bitter and just plain wrong – like a bonfire made of old tyres, used nappies, and cute little kitty cats.

Beside me, Alfie makes a choking sound. I assume that, like me, he's doing his best not to lose his lunch. Which, by the way, consisted of a single samosa and a couple of honey and tahini sandwiches, consumed what feels like half a lifetime ago. If this place didn't stink so bad, I'd be starving.

We're standing on a ridge of broken stone, looking out across a wide valley. Overhead, a crescent moon illuminates the thick layer of smog that shrouds the midnight sky. Down below, the valley floor flickers with tens of thousands of campfires, each one adding its smoke to the hot, foul air.

'Goblins,' Bruce growls. 'By the Seven Stones! If I still had my body, I'd show those dirtbags a thing or two.'

Alfie and I exchange a glance. Ever since Bruce took over that faery captain's mind, he's been a changed skull. He's fired up, literally. His eyelights blaze like a pair of orange flames.

And speaking of the faery captain . . .

'Bruce,' I say, carefully setting the skull down on a nearby boulder. 'You wouldn't ever . . . you know . . .' I hesitate. This feels like a delicate subject. 'That mind control thing. You wouldn't do that to one of us. Would you?'

'Certainly not!' The old skull's eyelights blaze red for a moment, then return to their normal orange.

'No, think about it, though,' Alfie says, and we both stare at him. 'I mean, you're a fountain of knowledge, right, Bruce? A receptacle of . . . what was it again?'

'Arcane wisdom,' Bruce says.

Alfie nods. 'Exactly. I bet you know all kinds of super-amazing magical stuff.'

'Of course I do,' Bruce snaps.

'Well, then. Why don't you just take control of Wednesday's mind . . .'

What? Ew. I glare at Alfie.

He gulps and hurries on. 'Or . . . or mine. And then together, we could—'

'Sorry, chucklehead.' Bruce grins. 'The Hypnotic Touch of Dragomar is strictly for self-defence. I can only do it when someone touches me with hostile intent.'

'Oh.' Alfie looks disappointed.

'Plus, it's exhausting,' Bruce says. 'And kind of icky. So I'm afraid the two of you are simply going to have to figure this out for yourselves.'

'Okay, fine,' I say. And frankly, it's a relief to know we can keep hanging out with Bruce without having to worry about being converted into human jack-o'-lanterns. But that still leaves the question of what to do next.

We turn and stare out across the smog-shrouded valley.

'So,' Alfie says, pointing, 'I'm guessing that would be the Tower of Shadows.'

In the middle of the vast goblin encampment, an enormous tower rises from the blackened earth like a spear. At first, I think the top of the tower is hidden by the smog, but then I realise the truth. The tower's the source of the smog. It's a huge chimney, a monolith of black stone, belching out the thick plume of sickening haze that covers the whole valley – and, for all I know, this whole world.

'Yep,' Bruce says. 'That's the place.'

Alfie shifts uneasily from foot to foot. 'It looks kind of . . . intimidating.'

I'm with Alfie on this. The Goblin Realm is a grim and terrifying place. 'You're sure Grandpa's in there?'

'Of course I'm sure,' Bruce snaps.

'And we can't just, you know . . .' I make a vague gesture with my hand. 'Pop in and grab him?'

'Sorry, Apprentice,' Bruce says. 'There's an anti-portal shield surrounding the tower. Our only chance is to do it the hard way – straight through the front gate.'

I gulp. 'There must be a better way. A safer way. Isn't there?'

We spend the next five minutes brainstorming better, safer ways. Alfie has some terrific ideas involving stealth helicopters, anti-gravity zip lines and old-fashioned grappling hooks. None of which we have.

I square my shoulders and take a deep breath. 'Looks like the hard way wins.' And, with less than two hours left on Gorgomoth's hourglass, we'd better hope the hard way is also the fast way. 'Let's go.'

The pathway down to the valley is steep and narrow, strewn with boulders, drop-offs and ample opportunity for excruciating accidents. We descend in single file, dodging from boulder to boulder to avoid being seen. At the bottom, I pull out the invisibility cloak and Alfie wraps it around us while I hold Bruce. The world turns faint and shadowy as the magic takes effect. Side by side, we shuffle forward across the blackened earth, heading for the tower.

We've only been walking a few minutes when a dark shape looms from the shadows. It's a tall, scary-looking

figure with spiky black armour and glowing red eyes –
like Gorgomoth, only smaller and without the flames.
A goblin soldier. He's standing still as a statue, glaring
into the darkness, an enormous curved sword clenched
in his armoured fist.

My heart pounds as we creep past, but the sentry
doesn't see us. He doesn't even blink.

We're inside the camp now. Thousands of ugly black
tents bulge from the ground like puffballs. The whole
place is swarming with goblin soldiers. They all look
like clones of the first sentry we saw, indistinguishable
in their black armour and horned helmets. Some bustle
around with armfuls of weapons and supplies, while
others sit beside roaring campfires, stuffing their faces
with spit-roasted meat and swilling wine from metal
goblets. Harsh voices and cruel laughter fill the air.

Sneaking through the camp is terrifying at first. It's
sweltering hot under the invisibility cloak, and my heart
pounds every time a goblin gets close or looks in our
direction. But, sheltered by the cloak, we soon get the
hang of sneaking and dodging past the soldiers. We
even get into a kind of rhythm. Sneak, sneak, dodge.
Dodge, dodge, hide. Hide, dodge, sneak.

After a while it's almost fun. But then it happens.

A trailing corner of the invisibility cloak snags on a
pyramid of spears, bringing the whole lot crashing to
the ground.

We freeze.

Four nearby goblins, who'd been standing around some kind of enormous six-legged beast roasting on a spit, drop their cooking thermometers and basting brushes and pull out their swords.

'Who's there?' the first goblin growls.

'Look!' The second goblin points at something on the ground.

My heart lurches. There, plain as daylight, are the prints of our boots – pressed deep into the thick layer of soot that coats the ground. With rising dread I check the feet of the goblins. Bare and clawed. Apparently, they have yet to discover the benefits of lightweight support and torsional cushioning.

'Intruders!' the third goblin roars. 'Sound the alarm!'

All the goblins within earshot drop what they're doing and rush in our direction, yelling, 'Intruders! Intruders!'

Within seconds the entire camp's in an uproar.

We sprint for the tower, clinging tightly to Bruce and each other beneath the invisibility cloak, like contestants in the world's longest and scariest three-legged race. Goblins chase after us, following the trail of footprints. Inevitably, our feet get tangled and we go sprawling. The invisibility cloak comes loose.

'There they are!' a goblin yells. 'Intruders!'

'Intruders? Where?' A second goblin bursts out of a tent and slams headlong into the first.

The two heavily armoured goblins crash to the ground with a sound like an earthquake in a saucepan factory. Soot flies everywhere.

'Inside, quick!' Alfie ducks past the distracted goblins and into the empty tent.

I follow him in, and we hunker down on a pile of filthy rags. I pull the cloak over us once more.

'You bumbleclunk!' the first goblin roars from outside. 'I had 'em!'

'Who are you calling a bumbleclunk?' the second goblin roars back. 'You're the bumbleclunk!'

There's the sound of an armoured fist crashing against a steel helmet.

'We can't stay here,' I tell Alfie. 'That goblin could come back any minute.'

'Well, we can't go out there. It's chaos!'

He's right. It sounds like the two goblins are tearing each other apart right outside.

I hold up the skull. 'Any suggestions, Advisor?'

Bruce's eyelights flash. 'Feed them to a sun-monster and use their back hair for basket-weaving!'

I shake my head. 'Top plan, but we're all out of sun-monsters right now.' I frown, thinking hard. 'We need a distraction. Something to draw them off.'

'A distraction?' Alfie shrugs off his schoolbag and pulls out his laptop and Alfie Junior. 'Hang on, I've got an idea.'

He sets the little purple robot on the ground, then flips open the laptop and starts tapping and clicking away, biting his tongue with concentration.

Heavy footsteps shake the ground outside the tent.

'That'll teach that bumbleclunk to call a guy a bumbleclunk,' a goblin voice mutters. 'Yeah, good luck finding your other leg, buddy!'

'He's coming back!' I hiss at Alfie.

'Almost there,' he whispers.

An armoured hand draws back the tent flap. The goblin looms in the doorway.

We're out of time.

CHAPTER 24

I quake under the invisibility cloak as the goblin enters the tent. He may not be able to see us, but I have a horrible feeling the pile of rags we're sitting on is actually his bed. We're just one nap away from disaster.

Alfie clicks the *Go* button, and Alfie Junior springs into action. The little purple robot zips out from under the cloak and races across the tent floor. It zooms between the startled goblin's feet and out into the night, beeping a merry tune.

'Intruder!' The goblin rushes out of the tent, roaring at the top of his lungs.

'Go, Alfie Junior!' Alfie yells, jumping up and down with excitement.

I clap my hand over his mouth.

The sound of Alfie Junior's whistling fades, drowned

out by the thunder of goblin feet as every goblin in the area stampedes after the little robot.

We wait for the stampede to pass, then peek out through the tent flap.

Not a goblin in sight.

'Now's our chance,' I whisper. 'Let's go.'

We arrange ourselves under the invisibility cloak once more, then hustle out of the tent and head for the tower as fast as we can. Not only have all the goblins rushed off to join the chase for Alfie Junior, but their mad stampede has stirred up the soot, so we don't have to worry about footprints. Although I am a little concerned about breathing.

After a few minutes of determined shuffling, we reach the tower.

I look up – and up – and up some more. This thing is absolutely enormous, a colossal smokestack the size of a skyscraper.

Directly ahead, an arched gateway big enough for a pair of double-decker buses gapes in the side of the tower. Dim orange light flickers from somewhere deep inside the shadowy opening.

We creep as close as we dare, then huddle in the shadows to catch our breath.

'That's weird,' Alfie whispers. 'I don't see any guards.'

I feel a surge of excitement. 'They're all off chasing Alfie Junior. Now's our chance!'

'Ahem.' Bruce makes that annoying little throat-clearing sound of his.

'What now?' I ask.

Bruce clacks his teeth. 'You don't notice anything *unusual* about the gateway, Apprentice?'

I frown and stare at the gateway. I'm itching with impatience to get inside and rescue Grandpa – but by now I've spent enough time around Bruce to know better than to ignore his cryptic remarks.

Right then, a goblin comes charging up.

Alfie and I shrink down under the invisibility cloak.

'Intruders! Intruders!' the goblin yells.

I flinch, but the goblin hasn't spotted us. He's heading for the gate, presumably racing to raise the alarm.

'Intruders! Intruders! In—'

BOOM!

As the goblin reaches the gateway, there's a blinding flash of light and a violent explosion. The goblin flies backwards like he's been shot out of a cannon, then crashes to the earth like a stone.

Horrified, I stare at the gate. Now I know what to look for, I can see it. The faintest shimmer, barely more than a ripple in the air, stretches across the archway.

'What *is* that?' I ask.

'I'm so glad you asked,' Bruce says wryly. 'It's a Curtain of Forbidding. Invisible. Unbreakable. Impervious to magic. No living thing may pass.'

Suddenly a squad of forty or fifty fully armoured goblins come charging out of the gate, yelling, 'Intruders! Intruders!' They charge past their fallen companion without a glance and disappear into the distance.

I scowl at Bruce.

'Of course, it *can* be deactivated,' he admits. 'It wouldn't be much of a gate otherwise, would it?'

I roll my eyes. 'So how do we deactivate it?'

Bruce's eyelights go dark for a moment, then flicker back to light. 'I can't see through the Curtain. But these things are usually controlled from somewhere nearby. We need to get closer.'

Still invisible, we creep forward, moving as carefully and quietly as we can. Suddenly, there's a whirring sound and something smacks into my ankle, causing me to almost jump out of my skin.

'*Beep! Beep!*'

'Alfie Junior!' Alfie exclaims, snatching up the little robot and hugging it to his chest. 'I'm so glad you're okay.'

I stare at Alfie in amazement. 'How did he find us?'

'Too easy.' Alfie grins. 'I just programmed him to drive around like crazy for a few minutes, then follow the signal back to my laptop.' He gives the robot an affectionate pat. 'You were amazing, Alfie Junior. Wasn't he, Wednesday?'

I blink. Alfie's looking at me like he's waiting for me to say something, and I think I know what it is.

I clear my throat. 'He sure was.' I've never congratulated a robot before, but it feels like the right thing to do. A little awkwardly, I reach out and pat the robot's plastic dome. 'Great job, Alfie Junior.'

Alfie beams.

'All right, you two,' Bruce says. 'If you're done admiring your miracle of technology, maybe we can get on with the mission?'

We creep as close to the archway as we dare and peer through.

In a shadowy alcove a short way inside the gate, a goblin slouches beside a big brass lever set into the wall, staring dully at the floor.

'That's it,' Bruce says. 'That's the control.'

'But how are we going to get there?' Alfie groans. 'You saw what happened to that goblin. Zap! Pow! Goodnight!'

'What's the plan, Apprentice?' Bruce asks.

'I suppose we could wait for it to open again,' I say. But then I imagine what Grandpa must be going through, locked away in the depths of Gorgomoth's dungeon. According to Alfie's watch, we have one hour and six minutes left, and I can't leave him there a minute longer. Besides, those goblins could come back any second.

My jaw clenches. We've got to get inside, now.

'Maybe I can pull the lever from here.' I concentrate, drawing in the magic. *'Levitate.'* With a wave of my hand, I unleash the spell.

It's perfect. The spell ripples through the air, heading straight as an arrow for the brass lever.

Bloop!

The spell hits the Curtain of Forbidding like a pebble dropped into a pond. It's gone with barely a ripple.

'I did say it was impervious to magic,' Bruce reminds me.

Darn it. No magic, and no living things. How in the Nine Realms are we going to get through?

'Come on, Bruce,' I say. 'There must be something. Some . . . counter-spell or something we can use to shut this thing down.'

'Sorry, Apprentice. Not even Saranon himself could magic his way through a Forbidding of this calibre.'

I shake my head. 'Some receptacle of arcane wisdom you are. What about you, Alfie?'

He looks doubtful. 'I guess I could send Alfie Junior through . . .'

Of course! It's perfect. Alfie Junior's not a living thing, so the barrier won't affect him.

'Brilliant!' I say, but then I see the look on Alfie's face.

'But even if he got past the guard,' he says apologetically, 'there's no way he could jump high enough to reach that lever. Even at maximum speed, he'd need a ramp of at least . . .'

He trails off as I slump against the wall.

'There must be a way.'

Bruce sighs. 'We can't change the laws of magic, Apprentice.'

'And we can't change the laws of physics,' Alfie adds.

I bite my lip. Here I am with a magical genius on one side and a scientific genius on the other, and what have I got? Zip.

If only I could smoosh them both together into a single super-genius.

Wait a second . . .

'That's it!' I exclaim. 'Smoosh you both together!'

Bruce and Alfie stare at me like I'm bonkers.

Bubbling over with excitement, I explain my plan.

Bruce's eyelights glow with appreciation. 'Nice work, Apprentice.'

'Molten!' Alfie exclaims, clapping me on the back.

He sets the little robot down on the floor. I place Bruce carefully on top, then tie the skull in place with one of Alfie's belts.

'Ready, Bruce?'

'Born ready, Apprentice.'

I give Alfie the nod, and he taps the *Go* button. Alfie Junior zips forward and races towards the gateway.

As the unliving robot and the undead skull plunge through the Curtain of Forbidding, Alfie Junior lets out a triumphant whistle, and Bruce yells, *'Chaaaaaarge!'*

The guard goblin springs to her feet, reaching for her sword and looking wildly around for the intruder. Alfie Junior screeches to a stop directly in front of her.

'Avaunt, goblin!' Bruce growls.

'Who goes there?' the goblin asks, still looking everywhere but down at her feet.

'Oi!' Bruce yells. 'Metal mitts. Down here!'

The goblin looks down, does a double-take, and lets out a cruel bark of laughter. 'Begone, skull, before I smash you to smithereens.'

'Smash me?' Bruce sneers. 'You'll have to catch me first.'

He zips away, but thanks to Alfie's clever programming, Alfie Junior's moving much more slowly than usual.

The goblin lunges, snatching at Bruce and wrenching him free from the belt . . . then freezes.

Then she turns, walks mechanically back into the alcove, and flips the lever.

The Curtain of Forbidding winks out.

With Bruce's now-empty skull clutched in one hand, the goblin gives me a cheery wave. Her eyes twinkle with pinpoints of orange light. 'Mission accomplished, Apprentice. Now, let's go get Abraham.'

CHAPTER 25

The goblin, still clutching Bruce-the-skull, leads us through the dark, smelly corridors of the Tower of Shadows. It's cold down here, and I button my jacket.

The place is crawling with goblins and it stinks like the valley outside, only worse. Every time we come face to face with a bunch of goblins, I feel sure our rescue attempt is over. But each time a goblin stops us, Bruce-the-skull speaks through Bruce-the-goblin's mouth.

'Just escorting these prisoners to the Pit of Extreme Discomfort,' she says.

And the other goblin nods and lets us pass.

We walk and walk and it's taking way too long. We head deeper into the tower, down slimy stone steps and along dank, torchlit corridors, and down more slimy steps, and on and on until it feels like it's never going to end.

'Thirty-one minutes left,' Alfie reports.

Sweat breaks out all over me. It's not going to be enough.

It has to be enough. 'Are you sure you know where you're going?' I ask Bruce.

Bruce-the-goblin gives me a haughty look and leads the way down a particularly noxious spiral staircase.

Finally, when I'm absolutely convinced we're completely and utterly lost, Bruce-the-goblin stops outside an armoured door. It's criss-crossed with steel and studded with spikes the colour of burnt toast.

'The Pit of Extreme Discomfort,' I breathe.

Without waiting to think about what might be waiting for us on the other side, I reach out and grab the door's heavy steel knob. I twist. And push.

The massive door creaks slowly open.

Beyond the door lies . . .

Well. It's horrific.

It's some sort of kitchen, with a huge cluttered table in the middle and dusty pots and pans hanging from hooks on the roof. Down one side is a line of sinks, overflowing with unwashed dishes and dirty dishwater. Down the other side is a long bench, covered in crusty knives and greasy chopping boards and dried bits of half-prepared food. A bunch of goblins are working at the bench, wearing chef's hats and dirty aprons over their armour.

A chef with stringy blond hair hanging from his chef's hat looks up. 'Prisoners! You here for the sardine-and-strawberry cakes?' he barks. The badge on his apron says *Dungeon Catering*.

I shake my head, too disgusted to form words.

'Then buzz off,' he snaps. 'We're all out of liquorice jelly, and the eel sorbet isn't ready yet.'

I try not to retch. Poor Grandpa. I can only hope he's survived these conditions.

'My mistake,' Bruce-the-goblin says, sounding confused. 'Wrong room.'

We retreat, closing the heavy door behind us.

'Wrong room?' I repeat. 'Seriously?'

Bruce-the-goblin glares at me. 'Oh, well, excuse me if I haven't been able to map this entire architectural monstrosity in the five minutes we've been inside.'

Alfie checks his watch. 'Actually, we've got twenty minutes left, so it's been more like—'

'Don't tell me how long it's been,' Bruce-the-goblin snaps. 'The level of astral interference in here is shocking.' The golden lights in her eyes flicker. 'All right. If that's the kitchen, then that means the dungeon must be . . .' She points across the hall. 'Over there.'

She's pointing at an identical armoured door. On it is a crudely handwritten sign: *Pit of Extreme Discomfort*.

'Oh, yay,' I say. 'Thank goodness we brought you, O Fountain of Knowledge.' But deep down, I really am grateful to old Skully McSkullface.

Grandpa, we're coming! I brace for the terror of the dungeon, then push open the door.

The room is long and thin and lined with shelves. The shelves are stacked with jars and cartons. There are sacks of flour and piles of potatoes in the corners. Nets of garlic and onions hang from the roof. It doesn't look like a dungeon at all.

I roll my eyes at Bruce-the-goblin. 'Wrong room again?'

Alfie starts reading labels from a nearby shelf. 'Sausage donuts. Pickled chicken. Seaweed jam. Candied asparagus.' He shudders. 'This is awful.'

He's right, but we can't waste time on menu planning. 'Shall we try again?' I ask Bruce-the-goblin.

That's when the fireball explodes into a shelf, splattering what smells like seaweed jam everywhere. Bruce-the-goblin shrieks, throwing her hands up in the air. Bruce-the-skull flies up with them. The orange disappears from the goblin's eyes as soon as she loses contact with the skull. She takes one look down the row of shelves and shrieks again, running out the door as I dive to catch Bruce before he falls.

A fiery figure has appeared at the far end of the

narrow pantry. It towers above us, shining and horned, its eyes glowing red as embers.

Gorgomoth.

'Run!' Alfie yells.

Excellent advice. We turn to follow the goblin's example, but the pantry door slams shut in front of us. I try to wrench it open, but it's stuck.

A fireball explodes on another shelf. Green sludge and asparagus spears fly everywhere. Alfie yelps, diving for cover behind a shelf of pickled chicken.

I try the door again, but it's no use. I need two hands.

I handball Bruce to Alfie and use both hands to heave on the door.

It still won't budge.

Wait, what am I thinking? I call up a panicky blast of magic and cast the opening spell. *'Open!'*

It's just an ordinary door, and I'm sure my intention is clear, but the spell fizzles out like it's run into a Curtain of Forbidding.

'He's using a closing spell,' Bruce calls. 'Take cover!'

More great advice. I dive behind the nearest shelf as a fireball explodes into the door.

Great. We're trapped in a pantry with a fireball-happy madman and a lifetime's supply of seaweed jam. I'm fairly sure we're all going to die.

Another fireball shoots through the air, slamming into a flour sack. The sack erupts in an explosion of white that makes it hard to breathe. Either that or the stink of seaweed jam.

'Pathetic fools,' Gorgomoth booms. 'Did you really believe it would be so easy to enter the Tower of Shadows? You have walked right into my trap.'

I think about navigating the Realm of Lost Things, battling the laundry kraken, sneaking through the goblin camp, tricking the gatekeeper . . . I really want to point out that getting this far wasn't actually 'so easy'.

Unfortunately, there isn't time. Another fireball blasts into the door. One more explodes into a sack of potatoes. Another shatters about a million jars of pickles. The whole place stinks like vinegar and chips.

Darn it. I hate vinegar on my chips.

I try to catch Alfie's eye through the haze of flour and exploded potato.

More fireballs explode, one after the other. Doesn't this guy ever need to reload? Then I remember what Bruce said. *Unquenchable Fire.* Of course. Gorgomoth is armed with a fire that never goes out.

More fireballs, getting closer.

Hiding behind the shelves, I rack my brain for a cunning plan, but it's no good. There's no way I can get to the door without being blasted to smithereens.

Alfie and Bruce are in an even worse position. They're further from the door than I am, stuck behind a shelf loaded with so many jars of disgusting-looking pickles they're one fireball away from turning into a pair of deep-fried pickles themselves.

It's time to face the facts.

We're trapped.

CHAPTER 26

Gorgomoth knows he's got us beat. 'Step forward, apprentice-creature,' he commands. 'I have your master. Surrender the Stone of Passage, and you will not be harmed. You and your master will go free.'

'And me,' Alfie yells from behind the pickles.

'I beg your pardon?' Gorgomoth says.

'I want to go free too,' Alfie says. 'I've been in this adventure the whole way. And Bruce too, right Bruce?'

Bruce doesn't answer. He's either thinking really hard, or he's chosen this moment to reconsider his career as a know-it-all chatterbox.

Gorgomoth doesn't seem to care either way. 'All very interesting, but I have things to do. Jams to taste, civilisations to topple, sworn enemies to subject to endless torment.' He shoots three fireballs, punctuating his list of things to do. They slam into the door, one after the other. 'So kindly hand me the stone.'

While Gorgomoth's been planning his afternoon and shooting fireballs, Alfie's been frantically signalling to me. Trouble is, I don't have a clue what he's trying to say. He's pointing at the shelves, making butterflies with his hands, then tearing at what's left of his hair. I literally have no idea. Finally he shrugs and hurls Bruce across the corridor.

A fireball sails towards Bruce as he flies through the air, but I catch him just in time.

'Bicarbonate of soda,' the old skull gasps. 'And pickles.'

Oh, dear. It's so very sad. Bruce has obviously lost his mind. Metaphorically as well as literally. Some sort of battlefield flashback, no doubt.

But Alfie's still making butterflies with his hands, and I realise. They're not butterflies. They're bubbles.

But what use are bubbles? We're trapped in a pantry, not a carwash.

'Bicarb,' Bruce gasps again. 'And pickles. They're pickled in vinegar.'

Bicarb and vinegar, just like in science class. That's genius! The oldest trick in the book, but pure genius.

I search the pantry for bicarb. Alfie points across the gap to a huge stack of the stuff – bags and bags of it. Must be for all that sardine-and-strawberry cake.

My heart sinks. It's on a shelf halfway down the pantry, almost at Gorgomoth's feet. There's no way I can—

BLAM!

Another fireball explodes. 'The ring,' Gorgomoth demands.

I take a deep breath. Then another.

'Okay,' I yell. 'You win.'

I set Bruce down on a bag of parsley flakes. 'Sit,' I tell him. 'Stay.'

'What are you—'

'I'm coming out,' I call to Gorgomoth. 'I have the ring. Don't shoot.'

The fireballs stop.

'You can't!' Bruce hisses. 'You mustn't!'

Cautiously, I step out from behind the shelving, both hands in the air. On the finger of my right hand the Ruby Ring glitters.

'Traitor!' Bruce screeches. 'Oh, the shame. How will I ever face your grandfather?'

Now that I'm no longer cringing behind the shelves, I can see Gorgomoth clearly. He's enormous. Fire bristles from every inch of his black armour. I can see the greed in his eyes as he spots the Ruby Ring.

'I have the ring, Mr Gorgomoth, sir. Please, just give me back my grandpa.'

Gorgomoth laughs, a dark and scary sound that

shakes the pantry to its foundations. 'At last.' He cackles. 'Bring it here.'

I nod, keeping my eyes on the ground so I can gauge how far along the pantry I've travelled.

One shelf. Two. Three. One more shelf, and I'll be at Gorgomoth's feet.

I take the last few steps, and finally I'm standing at the Goblin King's feet. I stand straight and proud. 'Prepare for your downfall, Gorgomoth!'

And I wave my right hand sideways through the air.

Nothing.

Oh, come on.

'Pitiful apprentice!' Gorgomoth crows. 'You still haven't mastered the secret of—'

I slash again with the ring, and this time I make sure the sharp edges of the ruby cut deep into the bags of bicarb. The white powder tumbles out onto the ground.

At that exact moment, Alfie throws a jar of pickles at Gorgomoth's feet. The jar shatters, spilling vinegar everywhere. Ha! How's that for teamwork?

Suddenly the floor is alive, fizzing and hissing with foam as the bicarb reacts with the vinegar.

'Enough!' Gorgomoth screams. He shoots a fireball right at me. It's point-blank range.

I close my eyes.

He can't miss.

But when I open my eyes again, the fireball is gone and Gorgomoth is screeching. 'Unquenchable! It's supposed to be *unquenchable.*'

I grin, backing away as fast as I can. Thank goodness for science! And pickles. Bicarb and vinegar make carbon dioxide gas. The same gas they use in fire extinguishers. And the same stuff that's bubbling all over the floor. Perfect for putting out fires – and fireballs.

I throw bag after bag of bicarb at Gorgomoth's feet as I retreat. Alfie, who has sprinted closer, pours jar after jar of pickle vinegar into the mix.

Soon Gorgomoth is knee-deep in a fizzing mound of carbon dioxide bubbles. He roars with frustration as his fire flickers and dims.

'It's working!' I yell. 'Don't stop.'

Alfie and I pile on the ingredients, but Gorgomoth clenches his fists and bellows like a swamp dragon. We stagger back as the white-hot flames blaze up even hotter than before.

I toss more bags of bicarb, but now they're getting cooked in mid-air. Alfie's vinegar is evaporating faster than he can throw it.

It's not working. The Unquenchable Fire is simply too hot.

We need more ingredients – a lot more.

More ingredients. A light bulb goes off in my brain. That's it!

Just as Alfie's about to throw the final pickle jar, I grab his arm and drag him behind a shelf.

I take the lid off the jar and tear open the final bag of bicarb.

'Pitiful human children!' Gorgomoth booms. 'You have failed again. Now, hand me the ring – or feel my wrath.'

'Coming!' I yell. 'Just a sec.'

I take a deep breath and reach into my pocket.

It's still there.

I grin with triumph as I pull out the spiky green ball. It's the winkleberry, the one I found in the Realm of Slugs. The humble ingredient whose power lies not in its own properties, but in its ability to temporarily multiply other ingredients.

'Alfie, quick,' I say. 'What's the chemical formula for bicarb?'

He blinks at me in surprise. 'It's . . . um . . . sodium bicarbonate. $NaHCO_3$.'

'Got it. What about vinegar?'

'Um . . .' Alfie looks panicked. 'I forget.'

Nuts. I cast my mind back to Mrs Glock's chemistry lesson and try to picture the molecules she drew on the whiteboard.

Amazingly, it works. 'Acetic acid!' I exclaim. 'CH_3COOH.'

I close my eyes and concentrate. I know now that it's not enough just to tell the magic what you want it to do. You have to tell it how.

Just like a robot. One step at a time.

So here we go. Start with the vinegar. I picture the acetic acid molecule in my mind, with its two carbon, two oxygen and four hydrogen atoms. Then I do the same for the bicarb. One atom each of sodium, hydrogen and carbon, plus three oxygen atoms.

Once I've got the two molecules spinning in my head, I start assembling my spell. I use imaginary coloured blocks, just like the code blocks we use in robotics class. One coloured block to take a molecule of acetic acid and turn it into two identical molecules. Another block to double a molecule of sodium bicarbonate. And one more block, a winkleberry block, to repeat the whole thing, over and over again, forever.

A magical recipe for multiplying ingredients. Simple, right?

I concentrate on the spell until it's as clear and sharp as a crystal spear. Then, still holding the spell in my mind, I drop the winkleberry into the jar, follow it with a handful of bicarb, and slam the lid back on.

'Hey, Gorgo-brains,' I say, as I step out from behind the shelf. 'Quench this.'

I throw the jar.

As it spins through the air, I release the magic and whisper, '*Multiply.*'

My spell ripples out, even as Gorgomoth sends a white-hot fireball hurtling towards the jar.

They meet in the middle.

The jar explodes. Bubbles go everywhere, extinguishing Gorgomoth's fireball like a candle in a bucket of milk. With a rumbling hiss, more bubbles form, doubling and redoubling in a matter of seconds.

Gorgomoth shoots fireball after fireball at the bulging mass of foam, but my winkleberry-fuelled chain reaction can't be stopped. The mountain of bubbles breaks over Gorgomoth like a wave. The Unquenchable Fire winks out, and he disappears beneath the foam with a despairing cry.

The wave crashes onto the floor and surges towards us.

'Run!' I yell.

Too late. The foamy wave picks us up and carries us along like a pair of corks.

As the torrent washes us towards the locked storeroom door, I yell the opening spell again.

This time it works.

CHAPTER 27

As Alfie and I are swept out of the storeroom and down the corridor on a sea of vinegar-and-winkleberry-scented foam, I hurriedly cast a closing spell. The pantry door slams shut, cutting off the stream of bubbles and dumping us like driftwood onto the stone floor.

'That was brilliant!' I pick myself up from the puddle of foam. 'I guess we won't be seeing old Gorgo-dummy anymore.'

Then I see Alfie's face. His eyes bulge like golf balls as he stares over my shoulder.

I gulp. 'Ah, nuts. He's behind me, isn't he?'

Alfie nods.

'*Bwaaargh!*' a terrible voice roars.

I turn to face the towering figure rising from the foam.

It's Gorgomoth. I guess I wasn't quick enough with the closing spell.

The Goblin King's fire is out. His helmet and most of his armour are gone, and . . . ew.

I try not to retch. No wonder he's called 'Gorgomoth the Unclean'. His hair is unwashed, his teeth unbrushed. His skin is crusted with decades – or maybe centuries – of indescribable filth, the accumulation of a lifetime of terrible personal hygiene. I can even see chicken bones matted into his long, straggly hair.

'You!' he roars, pointing a taloned claw at me. 'You have extinguished my Unquenchable Fire! You will pay for this outrage!'

He stomps forward, oozing a trail of filth.

The smell is indescribable.

Alfie and I back down the corridor, holding our noses.

'The ring!' Gorgomoth bellows. He flings out a hand and I feel a surge of dark power as his huge war hammer materialises in his fist. 'Give it to me!'

'Run, Wednesday!' Alfie steps in front of me and starts pelting Gorgomoth with soggy sausage donuts. 'Save the ring. I'll hold him off.'

But I can't run. Not without Alfie.

Gorgomoth glowers down at Alfie. 'Pester me not, insect,' he growls. 'I am in no mood for games.'

'Oh,' Alfie says, his tone apologetic. He swings his schoolbag to the floor with his left hand and grips the hilt of Grandpa's sword with his right. 'I'm sorry to hear that. Because I thought you might be in the mood for a game of . . . *Sword of Fury!*'

This time, the three-foot blade really does glide from its sheath with a deadly whisper of steel. I feel a keen, bright pulse of magic as the cryptic runes etched into the blade flicker to life.

Gorgomoth's eyes go wide and a flash of uncertainty crosses his grungy face. 'The Sword of Reckoning!'

Alfie grins and shifts the sword into a two-handed grip. The great blade burns with fierce green light.

'Game on, bumbleclunk,' Alfie says, and springs to the attack. He sprints forward, kicks off the wall and leaps high into the air, sweeping the sword at Gorgomoth.

I've never seen him move so fast.

But Gorgomoth's fast, too. He flicks the hammer in a tight arc, the great weapon like a conductor's baton in his massive hand.

Sword meets hammer with a ringing crash of steel and a blinding flash of light.

I feel another exultant pulse of magic from the sword, and an answering surge of cold, dark power as Gorgomoth draws in his magic.

'Congratulations, insect,' Gorgomoth rumbles, glaring at Alfie. 'You have my attention. Now, die.'

He brandishes the war hammer high over his head, then slams it down like he's trying to pound Alfie into the ground like a fence post.

Alfie dodges the hammer just in time. It smashes into the floor like a pile-driver, cracking the stone and sending splinters flying.

'No, thanks!' Alfie says cheerfully. He sweeps the sword in a dazzling flurry of strokes, forcing Gorgomoth back down the corridor.

'You have some skill, insect,' Gorgomoth says. 'But you should know, I do not fear your sorcerer's blade.'

He spreads his arms wide, brandishing the hammer. Shadows swirl about him, and I feel another wave of dark power gather itself like a thunderstorm.

'Alfie!' I yell. 'Look out!'

Gorgomoth swings the hammer.

Alfie parries with the sword.

When the two weapons touch, a fork of black lightning leaps from the hammer into the sword with a sound like a thunderclap.

The explosion throws Alfie through the air. He slams into the wall and drops to the floor, the Sword of Reckoning clattering from his hand.

No!

I reach for the magic, preparing to unleash a blast of mystic fire. But Gorgomoth strides forward and grabs Alfie around the waist with one enormous hand.

Alfie kicks and struggles, but it's no use.

Gorgomoth holds Alfie close, using him as a human shield. I can't get a clear shot.

'Give me the ring,' he says, giving me a baleful glare. 'Or I will crush this pitiful human creature like a bug.'

I hesitate. If I give Gorgomoth the ring, he'll enslave the Nine Realms, just like he promised. No one will ever be free again.

But I can't let him hurt Alfie.

'Get out of here, Wednesday!' Alfie yells. 'Don't worry about me.'

Gorgomoth shakes him like a kitten.

There's a cracking sound and Alfie screams.

The sound cuts through me like a sword.

I rip the Ruby Ring from my finger and hold it out. 'Here. Take it.'

Gorgomoth seizes the ring and lets Alfie fall to the floor.

I drop to my knees beside him. 'Are you all right?'

'Minty fresh.' He tries to sit up but gasps and clutches his side. 'Except I think my ribs might be broken.'

Anger flares deep inside me, and suddenly my whole body's tingling with magical energy. I've never felt it this strongly before. It feels like my heart's about to burst into flame.

Gorgomoth holds up the ring in delight, then slips it onto his finger.

'At last!' he crows. 'The riches of the universe will be mine!'

He swipes the glowing ring through the air, opening

an inky black void, then reaches into the blackness and pulls out a fabulous golden crown, encrusted with jewels.

'The Crown of Azeroth! Plucked from the brow of King Narvid himself! Like picking an apple from a tree.'

He dismisses the portal with a flick of his fingers and puts on the crown.

I help Alfie to his feet. He gasps and presses his hand to his side, face pinched tight with pain.

'Okay,' I say to Gorgomoth. 'You've got your stupid ring. Now release my grandpa.'

'Pathetic, gullible fool,' Gorgomoth sneers. 'Abraham Weeks is my sworn enemy. I will never release him. He will slave in my Pit of Extreme Discomfort until the end of time. As will the two of you. Guards!'

He snaps his fingers and a squad of goblin soldiers comes rushing around the corner.

My jaw goes tight.

I'm so angry I can't think.

The magic stirs inside me, and this time I don't try to hold it in.

The world turns hazy.

My hands burst into flame. I raise them over my head, and suddenly I'm holding a white-hot globe of fire the size of a basketball.

Alfie staggers back, shielding his face with one hand, clutching his ribs with the other.

The ceiling cracks, and the stone floor starts to melt from the intense heat.

I don't even feel it.

With a scream of rage, I hurl the fireball at Gorgomoth.

Blazing like a supernova, it streaks through the air, straight at his ugly face.

Gorgomoth rolls his eyes and gestures with his left hand. The Ruby Ring glows and an inky black void opens in front of him, swallowing the fireball. He gestures again, and the void collapses.

'Nice try, *Apprentice*,' he sneers. 'Your master couldn't defeat me. What makes you think you can?'

It's a fair question, and I don't have an answer. I put everything I had into the fireball, and it wasn't enough. I feel emptied out, drained, like I've just run a marathon while carrying the Empire State Building on my back.

Alfie does his best to catch me as I fall. 'Wednesday! Are you all right?'

'I'm sorry,' I whisper. 'It didn't work.'

Alfie shakes his head. 'Are you kidding? That was *amazing*. Your hair! It went all . . . floaty! And your eyes, they were all like . . . raaah!' He makes a scary face. 'And then the fireball! Whoosh! Pow! Blam!'

'Enough of this foolishness.' Gorgomoth snaps his fingers. 'Seize the prisoners.'

Two of the goblin soldiers clank forward and drag Alfie and me to our feet.

Gorgomoth's gaze falls upon the Sword of Reckoning, lying on the floor where Alfie dropped it. Its light is out and it lies dark and quiet upon the stone.

Gorgomoth's red eyes glitter with greed. He takes a step, then hesitates. He narrows his eyes, staring at the sword, then smiles.

'And bring me that sword,' he orders.

The other soldiers shrink back, eyeing each other nervously.

'Well?' Gorgomoth scowls at them. 'I certainly hope I don't need to remind you which one of us is the evil overlord around here.'

A tall, skinny soldier clears his throat, the sound muffled inside his cavernous black helmet. 'Begging your pardon, O Unclean One.' His voice drops to an apprehensive whisper. 'But isn't that . . . the Sorcerer's Blade?'

Gorgomoth frowns. 'What of it?'

'They say it's cursed, lord.'

The Goblin King grins, showing a mouthful of rotten teeth. 'Do they.'

'Yes, lord. They say it's death to touch it.'

'Nonsense!' Gorgomoth booms. 'Nought but foolish superstition. I order you to bring it to me at once.'

Trembling, the skinny soldier steps forward. He reaches for the sword, then pulls his hand back, flicks his eyes to Gorgomoth, and reaches again.

As his hand closes around the hilt, there's a flash and a sizzling sound. The soldier straightens bolt upright, then drops like a felled tree. He crashes to the ground and lies stiff as a board, motionless apart from a spasmodic twitch in his left foot.

'There, you see?' Gorgomoth booms. '*Death to touch it*, indeed. He's clearly still alive.'

The fallen goblin twitches again and lets out an eerie, high-pitched giggle.

Alfie and I exchange a horrified glance. Bruce wasn't joking when he said the sword doesn't like people. And apparently it likes goblins even less.

Gorgomoth ignores his fallen minion. 'You two, bring the prisoners,' he snaps, pointing a talon at the two soldiers holding Alfie and me. 'The rest of you . . .' He pauses and sweeps the remaining soldiers with a red-eyed glower. 'Bring the sword.'

The soldiers eye each other uncertainly. 'But how, lord?' one of them asks.

Gorgomoth rolls his eyes and strides away. 'Surprise me.'

The two soldiers clutching our arms hustle us along after him.

Gorgomoth stomps down the winding corridors until he reaches an enormous pair of iron doors, flanked by a pair of goblins.

The goblins salute and open the doors. Hellish orange light streams out, along with a blast of terrible heat. Gorgomoth goes through the doorway, and the soldiers drag us in after him.

'Ah!' Gorgomoth inhales deeply and sighs with satisfaction. 'Behold, my Pit of Extreme Discomfort. Breathtaking, isn't it?'

I look around. The Pit of Extreme Discomfort is a vast cavern, hewn from the living rock, deep below the Tower of Shadows – and, incidentally, nowhere near the kitchens. A huge pit yawns in the middle of the cavern floor, red-hot lava boiling deep within. Hungry flames shoot high into the air, and a pillar of dense black smoke rises out of the pit and up through a grated opening far above.

The heat is unbearable, and the smell's right up there for the Goblin Realm's Stink of the Year Award. Breathtaking is right.

The rest of the cavern is filled from floor to ceiling with enormous piles of garbage. In the lava's fiery glare, thousands of exhausted faery prisoners trudge endlessly, watched over by an army of grinning goblins.

Each prisoner picks up an armful of trash from one of the piles, carries it to the pit, and flings it over the edge, then trudges wearily back for more.

'Bring forth the sorcerer!' Gorgomoth booms.

The nearest guard-goblin knuckles his forehead and hurries away.

Minutes later he returns, leading a dishevelled figure. It's Grandpa.

CHAPTER 28

Grandpa's robes are tattered and his beard is singed, but his face is hard and determined. His eyes blaze as he glares at the Goblin King.

'You're wasting your time, Gorgomoth. You may keep me here for a thousand years, but the Ruby Ring will never be yours. My apprentice will see to that.'

Gorgomoth gives him an evil grin. 'Apprentice, you say?'

He snaps his fingers, and the goblin guards drag me forward into the light.

Grandpa goes pale.

'Behold!' Gorgomoth booms. 'I have triumphed.' The Ruby Ring glitters on his grubby finger like the eye of a serpent. 'Your plan has failed. I have the Stone of Passage. And I have your apprentice, too.'

Alfie winces as he pulls his arm out of the guard-goblin's grip. 'Don't forget me, you smelly old bumbleclunk!'

Gorgomoth ignores him. I try not to feel sick as he spits on the ring and gives it a polish.

'Wednesday!' Grandpa hurries over and kneels in front of me as Gorgomoth preens in triumphant delight. 'Are you all right? What happened to your eyebrows?'

'I'm all right, Grandpa.' I give him a hug, but suddenly it all comes pouring out. 'I'm so sorry about the ring. I couldn't get it to work, and then I accidentally sent it to the laundry, and then . . .'

Tears prick my eyes. I blink and look down at the floor. 'I've ruined everything, haven't I?'

'No, Wednesday.' Grandpa reaches out and gently lifts my chin. His soot-stained face is kind and sad. 'You have followed your heart down a difficult road. No master could ask for more.' Then he smiles. 'Nor any grandfather.'

Okay, give me a second.

I blink some more and take a couple of deep breaths.

'Oh, how touching,' Gorgomoth sneers.

I glare at him, then brush away my tears and turn back to Grandpa. 'What about you?' I ask. 'Are you okay? This place is horrible.'

'Well, yes. It has been rather a trial, what with the heat, and the smell, and Gorgomoth's constant gloating. And the food is awful.' He makes a face. 'Who ever heard of eel sorbet? But never mind me. I'm just glad you're safe.'

Alfie coughs. 'Broken ribs over here, people.'

'Oh tut,' Gorgomoth says. 'Poor tootums.'

'He's hurt,' I tell Grandpa. 'Can you help him?'

'Alas, the Unclean One has neutralised my magic.' Grandpa holds up his wrist, where a sturdy iron bracelet is clamped. 'But I should be able to make him more comfortable.' He gently checks Alfie's ribs, then tears a long strip of fabric from his robe. 'Well met, young Alfie,' he says, glancing at the frizzled wisps of hair poking out from under Alfie's stained and battered bucket hat. 'It appears my granddaughter is not the only one with a tale to tell.'

Alfie nods. 'I'll say! You should have seen the way we—' He breaks off, wincing as Grandpa winds the strip of fabric firmly around his chest.

Gorgomoth sniggers.

'I see someone has extinguished Gorgomoth's Unquenchable Fire,' Grandpa observes.

Gorgomoth stops sniggering.

Alfie grins. 'That was us!'

Grandpa raises his eyebrows. 'Indeed? You must tell me how you accomplished the feat.'

'Well—'

'Enough chitchat!' Gorgomoth booms. 'Guards! Bring forth another anti-magic bracelet.'

One of the goblins steps forward with an iron bracelet like the one on Grandpa's wrist.

Gorgomoth grins. 'No more fireballs for you, Apprentice.'

Grandpa looks at me in astonishment. 'You conjured a fireball? On purpose?'

'You bet she did!' Alfie beams proudly. 'She nearly took his head off.'

Before the goblin can put the bracelet on my wrist, another guard comes running up. 'Pardon the interruption, O Unclean One, but we found this among the prisoners' effects.'

At first it looks like the goblin's hands are empty, but then there's a telltale ripple in the air, and I realise he's holding the invisibility cloak.

Gorgomoth's eyes go wide. 'Can it be?' He snatches the cloak with his filthy hands. 'It is! The Unseeable Robe of Malazar! By my beard!' he crows. 'With this ring and this cloak, I shall be invincible! My armies shall cover the Nine Realms with a new darkness. I may even start my own reality show.'

The Goblin King does a grotesque happy dance. 'See, old man?' He waves the ring and the cloak in Grandpa's face. 'Your humiliation is complete. Your foolish apprentice has delivered both your greatest treasures into my keeping.'

Guilt stabs me like a rusty blade. What have I done? I wanted to help, but I've made things much, much worse.

I wanted to save the world. Instead, I've doomed it.

Grandpa squeezes my shoulder. 'You're wrong, Gorgomoth.'

'Am I, indeed?' Gorgomoth sneers. 'The look on your apprentice's face tells me otherwise.'

Grandpa draws himself up to his full height. Even disarmed, imprisoned and stripped of his magic, there's something dignified about him. Something ancient and noble and . . . I don't know. Fierce.

How come I never noticed that before?

My grandfather looks at me and his eyes gleam with pride. 'Do not underestimate her, Gorgomoth,' he says. 'She has always been blessed with the power to surprise. She has extinguished your Unquenchable Fire, and I warn you, she can defeat you with a single word.'

'A single word? Ha!' Gorgomoth lets out a bark of phlegmy laughter. 'That is an epic boast, even for you, old charlatan.'

I have to say, I'm with the Goblin King on this one. I mean, I appreciate the vote of confidence, but how in the Nine Realms am I supposed to defeat the most evil sorcerer of the age with a single word?

'It is no boast,' Grandpa replies calmly. 'She has already learned everything she needs to know.'

'Oh, indeed? How terrifying.' Gorgomoth looms over me, then pretends to shrink back in fear. 'Look at me, I'm shaking.'

Cruel laughter fills the air as the goblin soldiers slap each other on the back and enjoy my humiliation. I do my best to ignore them. Right now I'm trying desperately to think of whatever awesome word of power Grandpa seems to think he's taught me.

Saranon? Winkleberry? Underpants?

Honestly, I've got nothing. Even if Grandpa had taught me something like that – and I know for a fact he hasn't – if it didn't work for him during the fight in the swamp, it's never going to work for me now.

Gorgomoth gives Grandpa a snaggle-toothed grin. 'Enjoy your thousand years of servitude, old man. I'm off to conquer the universe.' He swirls the invisibility cloak around his shoulders and his body vanishes, leaving his head floating in mid-air like the world's nastiest party balloon.

Anger knifes through me at the thought of Grandpa's precious cloak being dirtied and stained by the Unclean One's rancid coating of nauseating filth. It's just come straight from the laundry, for crying out loud.

Okay, that's it. I'm taking this guy down. I'm not going to be responsible for the end of the world. I'm just not, okay?

Not today.

I take a deep breath and reach for the magic. No sparks burst out, nothing explodes. I'm angry, but I'm in control. Which is great, but I still don't know how I'm going to defeat Gorgomoth.

I've got to think. What did Grandpa say before?

He said I can defeat Gorgomoth with a single word. Okay, that still seems pretty unlikely.

He said I've already learned everything I need to know.

But that can't be right, can it? I may have mastered levitation and taught the Globe of Tarimos some nifty tricks, but there's still so much to learn.

So, what else did Grandpa say? Something about the power to surprise?

Well, let's hope he's right about one that. Because if I can defeat Gorgomoth now, it'll be the biggest surprise in the history of the universe.

I mean, come on. A single word? The last time I made something surprising happen with a single word was . . .

The solution hits me like a bolt of lightning. It's so simple.

CHAPTER 29

'Gorgomoth!' My challenge echoes around the cavern.

All the goblins and prisoners stop what they're doing and look in my direction.

'Be silent, foolish child,' the Goblin King commands, his revolting head sticking out from the now-equally-revolting cloak. 'Unless you wish to beg for mercy?'

'Hardly.' I assume my wizarding pose and muster up every scrap of magic I can gather. Let's hope it's enough.

'In the name of the Nine Masters, I charge you,' I intone.

The Goblin King sneers. It's the same spell Grandpa used against him back in the swamp. The one that didn't even scratch his armour.

'With the Seven Stones of Saranon, I bind you.' I raise my hand towards Gorgomoth, as if preparing to blast him with magical fire.

Gorgomoth looks on mockingly. Some of the goblin soldiers laugh, but the ones standing closest to Gorgomoth shuffle back a step or two.

'By the power of Undilion, I command you . . . begone from this place!'

'Oh, please.' Gorgomoth says, wiping his disgusting hands on the cloak. 'Just stop. You're embarrassing yourself.'

'Oh, yeah?' I smile.

And then I say the word.

'*Laundry.*'

There's a popping sound and the familiar ripple of a spell being cast. A shower of green sparkles fills the air.

Gorgomoth reaches out from under the cloak to swat at the sparkles. 'What is this devilry?' The sparkles swirl thicker and faster, twisting around the Goblin King and lifting him into the air. 'No! Impossible!' His legs pop into view as he kicks and struggles, but the magic holds him tight. 'You can't defeat me! You're just an apprentice!'

'You're wrong, Gorgomoth.' I lift my chin and prop my hands on my hips. 'I'm not just an apprentice.'

I glare around me at the terrified goblin soldiers. Then I sneak a glance at Grandpa and give him a wink. I know he'll like this next bit. After all, a sorcerer's introduction is her most powerful weapon.

'I told you before,' I say in a loud, clear voice. 'I'm Wednesday Elizabeth Weeks. Now, begone!'

I snap my fingers.

'Noooooooo!' Gorgomoth wails in despair as the tornado of green sparkles closes around him.

There's a flash of green light and a puff of lavender-scented smoke. When the smoke clears, the Goblin King is gone.

After all, that's how it goes.

Nothing can stop faery magic when there's laundry to be done.

The goblin soldiers stare at me, wide-eyed and trembling.

I glare at them and raise my hand like I'm preparing to send them into oblivion with a snap of my fingers.

'Boo!' I say.

As one, the soldiers drop their swords and sprint for the exit. With a roar, the faery prisoners drop their burdens of garbage and chase after them.

In less than a minute, I'm alone in the dungeon with Grandpa and Alfie. I step forward to the place where Gorgomoth was taken and pick up the white cardboard ticket that's lying on the floor.

LAUNDRY FAIRY DRY CLEANING

THE TOWER OF UNBEARABLE BRIGHTNESS (LEVEL 9)

THE FAERY REALM

I turn the card over. On the back it says:

WEDNESDAY ELIZABETH WEEKS

WITH THANKS FOR SERVICES RENDERED
(DEFEATING GORGOMOTH THE UNCLEAN, ANCIENT FOE
OF THE FAERY REALM, SAVING THE UNIVERSE, ETC.),
A NEW ACCOUNT HAS BEEN OPENED IN YOUR NAME.
YOUR CREDIT IS: UNLIMITED.

'Wow!' Alfie says, reading over my shoulder. 'Your own account. With unlimited credit! How cool is that?'

Before I can answer, there's another shower of green sparkles and the invisibility cloak pops out of thin air and lands in my arms, freshly laundered and good as new. At the same time, the Ruby Ring materialises on my finger.

A second ticket flutters to the ground. This one's handwritten.

Hey, Wednesday —
I thought you might need these.
Stay sunny!
Adaline
P.S. We're keeping that other dude.

It only takes me four tries to get the right spell to remove Grandpa's anti-magic bracelet, which he promptly stashes in the pocket of his robe. Alfie retrieves his backpack from a pile of goblin booty, and then we all head off in search of Bruce.

It doesn't take long to find him. He's back in the pantry, half-buried in parsley and stained a lovely bright green, which goes nicely with his orange **VISITOR** sticker, and with our own pickle-scented and foam-dusted outfits. Alfie starts to tell him what happened, but the skull doesn't seem in any hurry to hear about our incredible victory.

'Please,' he says, 'no details until I'm clean. Honestly, I feel like an Irish flag.'

'Hello, old friend,' Grandpa says. 'I'm surprised to see you here. I thought your fighting days were over.'

'Yes, well.' Bruce clears his non-existent throat. 'Naturally, as soon as I heard you were in danger . . . I mean . . . that is to say . . .'

I can't believe it. The old skull actually sounds embarrassed.

I lift him gently out of the parsley and peel the sticker off his forehead. 'He was amazing,' I tell Grandpa. 'We couldn't have done it without him.'

'That's right!' Alfie says enthusiastically. 'You should have seen him charge the gate.'

Grandpa looks stunned. 'He . . . charged the gate?'

Alfie grins. 'He sure did. Zoom! Whiz! Whack! Straight through the Curtain of Forbidding.'

'Astonishing,' Grandpa murmurs.

Bruce's eyelights brighten. 'I must admit, it's been good to get out of the house for a while. I haven't felt so alive in centuries. All the same . . .' He glances around the ruined pantry. The floor is littered with broken glass, pulverised asparagus and what I can only imagine must be squashed sausage donuts.

'Wise counsel, my friend,' Grandpa says. 'We should leave this place.' He leads the way out of the pantry, his stained and tattered robe trailing through puddles of foam and mounds of pickled chicken. I can't help feeling sorry for the Laundry Fairy Dry Cleaners when they receive their next consignment.

Grandpa strides along the corridor, his long legs setting a cracking pace. He seems to be looking for something, but I can't think what.

We turn a corner and see a mound of giggling, twitching goblins lying on the floor.

'Excellent,' Grandpa says. With a clank of steel, he rolls an armour-clad goblin aside and reaches into the pile. 'I see you brought my sword.'

The Sword of Reckoning thrums with power at its master's touch. Apparently those goblins never did figure out how to pick it up.

Grandpa holds the sword thoughtfully for a moment, then gives me a sideways look. 'How careless of me to leave that chest unlocked.'

Ah. My face goes hot.

I scramble for an explanation but before I can say anything, Alfie clears his throat and says, 'I found it in your box, sir. I hope you don't mind.'

'*You* did?' Amazement flashes across Grandpa's face. He raises his eyebrows at Bruce.

'I'm as surprised as you are, boss,' the old skull says. 'But it seems to have taken a real shine to the lad.'

'Astonishing.' Grandpa strokes his beard. 'Can there really be two?'

'Apparently,' Bruce says.

'Two what?' I ask suspiciously. 'What are you two talking about?'

Grandpa ignores me. 'But the boy has no magic.'

'Maybe that's the point,' the old skull replies.

Grandpa considers for a moment, then nods. 'We shall see.' With a well-practised move, he reverses the Sword of Reckoning and offers it to me, hilt-first. 'Touch the sword, Wednesday.'

Okay, seriously? Another test, after everything I've just been through? And this time there's not even meatloaf.

But I'm too tired to argue. I hand Bruce to Grandpa, then reach out and grasp the sword. Its well-worn leather grip is warm and smooth beneath my fingers. There's a faint tingle of power, a dull gleam from the runes on the blade, but nothing else. Not like when I drew the sword to fight the kraken, or when Alfie wielded it in battle against Gorgomoth.

I shrug and let go of the sword.

Grandpa nods. 'Now you, young Alfie.'

'Me?' Alfie's eyes go wide.

'Do not be afraid,' Grandpa says.

Alfie reaches out a trembling hand and touches the sword.

I don't know what Grandpa's expecting, but whatever it is, it doesn't happen. Just the same flutter of power, the same faint gleam.

'Now, both of you,' Grandpa says. 'Together.'

Alfie looks at me.

I shrug. Anything to get out of this smelly corridor. Together, we reach out.

The triumphant surge of power when our two hands grip the sword is like nothing I've ever felt before. The Sword of Reckoning flares with blinding emerald light along its entire length, and the runes etched into the blade blaze like letters of fire.

Grandpa gasps. 'By the Stones!'

'See, boss?' Bruce says smugly. 'I told you.'

I stare at the Sword of Reckoning. At our two hands gripping the hilt, mine and Alfie's, side-by-side. At the fiery letters gleaming on the blade like a promise of things to come. Suddenly my heart feels as light as a feather.

'What does it mean?' Alfie asks.

Bruce laughs. 'It means buckle up, chucklehead.' His eyelights gleam with satisfaction. 'You're going on an adventure.'

'Another one?' Alfie looks like he's about to burst with happiness. 'For real?' he whispers, and I shoot him a happy grin.

Two Protectors of the Realms? Sounds like twice the fun to me.

'For real,' I say.

'Excellent,' Grandpa says crisply, retrieving the sword. The green glow goes out and the fiery letters fade. He turns to me. 'Wednesday, you have the ring?'

I reach for the ring, to give it back to Grandpa, but he stops me.

'Kindly take us home,' he says.

My throat goes tight. So much for twice the fun.

Don't get me wrong – I'd love to go home. Even though explaining to Mum and Dad how I came to be out past 2am, having dinner with Alfie, is going to be tricky.

'Well?' Grandpa asks.

I gulp and watch the ring twinkle on my finger. Will he really want an apprentice who can't even conjure a portal?

'I'm not sure I can,' I say. 'I mean, I've never been able to . . .'

Bruce winks an eyelight at me. 'You've got this, Apprentice.'

'Totally,' Alfie says.

Bruce and Alfie's confidence is reassuring, but I'm still not convinced. Because it's not enough to tell the magic *what* to do. You have to tell it *how*. And I don't have the faintest clue how to open a portal between worlds.

On the other hand, how much do I know about the chemical properties of winkleberry juice, or the motors, gears and microchips inside a robot? Maybe those details aren't important.

Maybe all I need is one coloured block to open a doorway in this world, and another block to open a matching doorway back in our basement.

Can it really be that simple? I picture the spell in my mind, swipe my hand through the air and whisper, '*Open.*'

The inky void appears, shimmering and swirling in the air like an old friend.

Alfie cheers.

Grandpa smiles and bows his head. 'Well done, Apprentice.'

I smile back. Because, you know what? He was right all along. You really do draw the magic with your heart and shape it with your mind. It just took me a while to get my heart and mind onto the same page.

'Thanks, Grandpa,' I say.

Grandpa's smile fades. 'Wednesday, when in public, you really should address me as Master.'

I fold my arms. 'You know that's never going to happen, right?'

Grandpa sighs, but there's a twinkle in his eye. 'I know.'

'Ha!' Bruce guffaws.

I take Grandpa's hand on one side and Alfie's on the other. 'Let's go home.'

CHAPTER 30

One week later, Alfie and I are back in Mrs Glock's classroom. It's our final robotics class – do or die for me if I want to pass.

No one seems to remember Grandpa arriving in a puff of smoke, then whisking me and Alfie away into an inky black void. In fact, they don't seem to remember anything about the last robotics lesson at all. Although Mrs Glock does keep glancing at the place where the Harbour Bridge once stood, and then staring at me with a cool and somewhat thoughtful expression – like she knows there's *something* she should be mad at me about. And her hand keeps twitching towards her collection of fire extinguishers.

'Just past the second corner, people,' she reminds us. Then her eyes land on me, her lips pinch tight, and she adds, 'If you can.'

Nice. I move my right hand to my left wrist and absently play with the metal bracelet I'm wearing. I spin it round and around, like a good luck charm.

Of course, who needs a good luck charm when you can defeat Gorgomoth the Unclean, King of the Goblin Realm and most powerful sorcerer of the age? Who needs luck when you have science? And a little magic. I give the bracelet one last twist. As long as I'm wearing it, nothing can go wrong.

Alfie goes first. Thankfully, he remembers everything that happened on our quest. And Grandpa's agreed to let it stay that way. Even better, Grandpa covered for us. He told our parents it was his fault we were late, that he'd taken us out and lost track of time. And for some reason – a little reason that Grandpa likes to call amnesia – they believed him. Of course, all that magic hasn't affected Alfie's passion for maths and science. He's spent the last five minutes tapping away at his laptop, humming happily to himself. As soon as he hits the *Go* button, I see why.

Alfie Junior speeds through the maze even faster than last time, then turns to come back. But then it stops. For a second, I think the little purple robot has switched itself off, but then coloured lights start flashing all over it, like it's caught some kind of disco fever.

Alfie Junior blasts out a tinny drumroll, then starts to whistle at the top of its speakers. The tune is high-pitched and a little distorted, but familiar. I look at Alfie and he gives me a wink. Because his robot is whistling the tune to *I Once a Wandering Wizard Knew.*

Mrs Glock laughs and claps. 'Oh, how clever, Alfie!' And soon our whole class, even Mrs Glock, is bopping along to the wizarding world's worst country hit. From the seventeenth century.

It actually feels good.

The little robot finishes its song and we all cheer as it returns obediently to Alfie's side.

Everyone's grinning and puffing after their dance workout, especially Mrs Glock, who pulled some spectacular moves in the final chorus. But she has enough breath to say, 'Your turn, Wednesday.'

I nod. I knew this moment would come, and I'm ready. I give my bracelet one last twist, then turn to my laptop. Usually its screen would start fading in and out right about now, responding to the bursts of wild magic surging out of my body like static electricity.

But not today.

Today I'm wearing Gorgomoth's anti-magic bracelet – the one he used to prevent Grandpa from enchanting his way out of the Pit of Extreme Discomfort. With its new easy-release clasp – courtesy of a couple of paperclips and a little ingenuity – it's perfect for those occasions when I need to keep the magic at bay.

To tell you the truth, I'm not sure I actually need the bracelet anymore. Our classroom hasn't suffered a single blackout since Alfie and I got back from the Tower of Shadows, and I haven't felt the urge to set Colin Murphy's hair on fire in days. But it's handy to have a backup, just in case.

'It's working,' I whisper to Alfie. Then I hit the *Go* button.

My robot trundles forward and enters the maze. It's not nearly as fast as Alfie's, but it doesn't slow down or hesitate, and it never even *looks* like it's going to explode.

Mrs Glock's carefully pencilled eyebrows go up as my robot passes the second corner and keeps going. Before I know it, it's finished the maze. Mrs Glock stares at the fire extinguisher in her hand as if she's never seen it before. Then she sets it down on her desk and makes a note on her shiny black tablet. I can't be sure, but I think she's smiling.

'Well done, Wednesday,' she says warmly. 'Colin Murphy, you're next.'

Alfie gives me an under-the-desk high-five.

I did it!

Relief flows through me. I've passed robotics. And not only that, but I've managed a whole week of school without blowing anything up, setting anything on fire, or turning anybody into anything unnatural.

Maybe there's still a chance for me to—

Colin Murphy's robot spins on the spot and bursts into flame. My heart stops. No. You've got to be kidding. I thought I had this.

Then the lights flicker and a chill fills the air. At the same moment, all the laptops die. And I grin. My heart starts back up again. Because it's not me. It's him. And he's early.

Mrs Glock glares at the tall, cloaked figure standing at the back of the room. 'Excuse me!' she says, like she does every time this happens. 'Who are you? And what are you doing in my classroom?'

'Forgive the intrusion,' Grandpa says in his deep, smooth voice. 'I have come for my apprentices.'

'Molten!' Alfie cheers.

Mrs Glock frowns. 'Apprentices?'

Grandpa flings out a finger, pointing at me and Alfie in his dramatic, billowy-cloak way.

I roll my eyes.

I mean, seriously. This is the kind of stuff I have to put up with.

ACTIVITIES

Wednesday and Alfie encounter many obstacles as they travel the Nine Realms. They must put their heads together to come up with clever solutions, combining what they know of the world of magic with real-world STEM principles.

STEM stands for Science, Technology, Engineering and Maths. There are many STEM concepts found in this book which you can explore, including

- chemical reactions
- combustion
- Faraday cages
- robotics
- coding and computer programming
- mathematics involving pi.

Following are some fun STEM activities you can try at home or in the classroom.

MISSION: GET PRIMED FOR PRIME NUMBERS

A prime number is any positive number that is divisible only by itself and one. Alfie has memorised loads of prime numbers, but just how easy is that? What are the first ten prime numbers? Is 1 a prime number? Can you recite all the prime numbers below 50 in under 20 seconds?

MISSION: YOUR A-MAZE-ING HOUSE

While trapped in the laundry maze in the Realm of Lost Things, Wednesday uses the *wall follower* method of maze navigation to try to find her way out. For lots of mazes (but not all of them), wall following is a simple way to explore every part of the maze.

Using a pencil, try using the wall follower method on the maze below, starting at the top star:

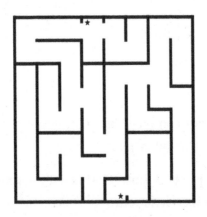

If you want to practise this method some more, you can find maze generators online or draw your own maze on a sheet of graph paper.

You can also use the wall follower technique to explore your own house.

What to do:
1) Start in any room of your house and pick a wall.
2) Put your hand on the wall and start walking.
3) Follow the wall around your house. When you get to a doorway, go through it and keep following the same wall. You don't have to touch the wall the whole time – if something's in the way, like a bed or a cupboard, just skip past it and keep following the wall.
4) Keep going until you end up where you started.

How did you go? Did you get to every room in your house? If there were some places you didn't get to, why was that? Does it matter if you use your left or right hand?

MISSION: JUG CHALLENGE OF DOOM

To escape from Certain Doom in the Fullonica vault, Wednesday and Alfie had to measure volumes of liquid from 1 to 8 units, using only a 5-unit and a 3-unit jug. You can recreate this jug problem with just a few items.

You will need:

- 1 x empty 1-litre bottle (a milk bottle works well)
- 1 x empty 600 ml bottle (we suggest a water bottle)
- plastic bowl (about 1-litre capacity)
- digital kitchen scale
- permanent marker
- water

What to do:

1) Use the kitchen scale to measure exactly 1000g of water into the 1-litre bottle (remember to zero the scale after you place the empty bottle onto it).

2) Use the permanent marker to carefully mark the level of the water on the outside of the bottle, then label the container with the number '5'. This is your 5-unit jug (each unit is 200g).

3) Now measure exactly 600g of water into the 600ml container.

4) Mark the level as before and label this bottle with the number '3'. This is your 3-unit jug.

5) Place the plastic bowl onto the kitchen scale.

Your challenge:

Using only the '5' and '3' jugs, can you measure exactly 4 units of water (800g) into the bowl? To avoid Certain Doom, your result needs to be between 750g and 850g.

MISSION: UNBELIEVA-BUBBLE

Wednesday, Alfie and Bruce use 'the oldest trick in the book' to quench Gorgomoth's Unquenchable Fire. They mix vinegar (which is an acid) with bicarb soda (which is a carbonate). When the two combine, they react to produce bubbles of carbon dioxide gas – the same gas that's used in some fire extinguishers.

You will need:
- vinegar (acetic acid)
- bicarb soda (sodium bicarbonate)
- a plastic container
- safety glasses
- adult supervision.

(Note: This experiment can be messy, so do it outdoors or in a laundry sink.)

What to do:
1) Put on the safety glasses.
2) Pour half a cup (125ml) of vinegar into the plastic container.
3) Drop in one tablespoon of baking soda.
4) Stand back!

Extension: What happens if you use cold vinegar from the fridge? What happens if you use frozen vinegar?

ACKNOWLEDGEMENTS

Thanks are due to many, many people who helped turn this project from a just-for-fun story into the book you're holding in your hand.

To Jeanmarie Morosin, Sophie Mayfield, Rebecca Hamilton and the rest of the Hachette team, for falling in love with our not-always-perfect heroine. Thank you for taking us on as your apprentices.

To Danielle Binks and Jacinta di Mase, for being our fountains of knowledge and arcane wisdom.

To Chris Wahl for his jaw-droppingly awesome cover art, so good it made Denis cry.

To our fellow squibbies from the Society of Children's Book Writers and Illustrators. Every adventurer needs a band of faithful companions. You guys are ours.

To Jessica Wyld, for sprinkling us with faery magic during our photo shoot.

To Nadia L. King, Shirley Marr and HM Waugh, for hash browns, hugs and general Faux Four hijinks.

To Iman, Salman, Abdullah and Ibrahim, for your advice and creative, clever thinking.

To the team at Mount Kaputar National Park for their conservation of the real pink slugs, which are found only in the mists of an extinct Australian volcano.

To the Children's Book Council of Australia, and especially to Jan Nicholls, for your tireless and voluntary advocacy for children's literacy.

To our parents, for always supporting our creativity, even when it's accompanied by inexplicable fireballs or extraordinary hair.

To Nic and Heath and Neets, for decades of unquenchable love and adventure.

To Lauren and Matthew, for serving as guinea pigs for baffling quantities of dad-humour, and to Fergus and Rory, for testing out kraken-loads of STEM shenanigans.

To Connie, for putting up with Denis's nonsense all these years. And to Doug, for all those long walks on the beach (and the super-awesome ruby ring).

And finally, to you: Wednesday's new friends. To all the readers, booksellers, teachers, librarians, bloggers and cheerleaders who have roamed the Nine Realms with us. We're grateful, we're bursting, we want to meet you and talk books and magic and science all day long.

Let's conquer the universe together!

THE NINE REALMS ARE IN TROUBLE AND
IT'S UP TO WEDNESDAY AND ALFIE
TO STEP IN!

COMING SEPTEMBER 2021